BLOOD OF THE COVENANT

THE CHAOS MAGES II

ALEX STEELE

STEEL FOX MEDIA LLC

BLOOD OF THE COVENANT

THE CHAOS MAGES BOOK 2

ALEX STEELE

Blood of the Covenant
All rights reserved.

First edition, September 2018
Version 1.0, September 2018
ISBN 978-1-7324518-4-1

The True Chaos Mages

A big thank you to my ART (Advanced Reader Team) AKA Berserker Reader Team. They helped turn a good book into a great one.

Chris Christman II, David M., Denise King, Karen Hollyhead, Larry Diaz Tushman, Laura Rogers, Liz Christensen, Penny Campbell-Myhill, Rob Hill, Samantha Rooney, Terri Adkisson, Tom Ryan

I also want to thank my editors, The Ranting Raven and Sarah Burton at An Avid Reader Editing. Without going into personal details, I will say that Sarah went through a trying time during the editing of this book. I would ask that you keep her in your thoughts and prayers.

"The blood of the covenant is thicker than the water of the womb."

CONTENTS

ONE

F ire rained down from above, streaking across the
sky like fireworks. Glass shattered overhead. A
man and a woman ran from the shrieking monster that
loomed above the city. We were running out of time –
and out of options.

I sheathed my katana and raced forward, weaving
through smoldering cars and craters the size of a bus.
Swift was a few meters ahead of me, her red trench coat
trailing behind her like a matador's cape.

The phoenix leaped into the sky, its wings unfurling
in a blaze of oranges and reds. It was *huge*. The wings'
tips crashed through skyscrapers, searing glass and
metal with the unbearable heat. Protective runes flared
but were burned through instantly, shattering the glass.

Whoever had resurrected it wanted anarchy. They
wanted to destroy -- nothing more, nothing less. A

phoenix couldn't be controlled, no matter how strong the mage. It was a weapon of mass destruction that would kill the summoner as soon as a random passerby.

We were not prepared for this.

I picked up my pace, jumping up onto the back of a half-crushed car and hop-stepping my way onto the precariously leaning roof of a liquor store. Chief Bradley was supposed to have given us the weekend off, but no. He had to send us after some idiot that stole the ashes of a phoenix, then summoned the monster. I should have been sleeping like a baby right now, not fighting for my life and the fate of New York City. *Technically*, I was still banned after that unfortunate incident where I blew up part of the Met, but the mayor was desperate, and we were the only mages available for such an emergency.

"Come and get me, you ugly ass carpet bird!" Swift shouted, waving her mace like a baton. Carpet bird didn't even make sense. She must be getting tired.

The phoenix shrieked, insulted nonetheless, and dove at Swift. She swung her mace, pink magic flaring all around her. It hit the creature square on the beak, but didn't stop the phoenix's momentum. It shoved her back, crumpling the ground beneath her feet as she tried to resist the onslaught.

I took a running leap and aimed for its back, drawing my katana as I flew through the air. This thing was the size of a teenage Godzilla. It couldn't fully extend its wings in the street, but it could rear up straight. When it did, the plumage on the top of its head made it taller than the ten-story building across from us. I wrapped both hands around the handle of my sword and stabbed down as my feet hit slippery feathers. The blade sank into the phoenix's meaty shoulder.

The phoenix reared back with an angry shriek, and my feet flew out from under me. It twisted its head around, snapping at the unwanted passenger currently stabbing it in the neck. The back of the wing smacked me, almost breaking my grip on the katana.

"Distract it!" I shouted down to Swift.

"I'm trying!" Swift shouted back. "But you shouldn't have jumped on its back, you idiot!"

I ground my teeth together and tried to drag myself farther up, but the bird twisted and shook. I caught a glimpse of its fury in one beady, black eye. This thing had seriously woken up on the wrong side of the nest.

A sudden burst of pink light blazed up underneath the bird. It shrieked in pain and launched upward, twisting in the air until my feet were dangling over the city. The katana slipped once, then tore free, and we both fell.

I'm not saying I screamed, but the noise that came out of my throat wasn't manly.

Slapping my hand against the runes engraved on my

katana, I cast a shield rune just in time to avoid splattering my brains all over the asphalt. The magic protected me, but the sudden stop was still jarring. I hastily canceled the rune and climbed out of the small crater. My suit was singed, my head was pounding, and the acidic blood of the phoenix had burned my hands.

The phoenix dove at Swift. She swung her mace upward, catching it on the beak like an uppercut. I ran toward them, frantically trying to come up with another plan of attack. What we were doing wasn't even slowing it down.

I sheathed my sword. It was time to fight fire...with ice. Pulling on the magic churning inside me, I focused it, shaping it to my will. With a deep breath, I thrust my palms toward the phoenix. Bright, white magic soared toward it, hitting its vulnerable underbelly. Ice flowed over the bird, creeping along its wings and up over its face.

Swift charged in immediately, hitting its leg and knocking it off balance. The phoenix shrieked in anger, and fire erupted from its beak. The pillar of flame shot up into the sky.

The ice immediately began melting, running off the fiery, piece-of-shit pigeon like a waterfall. Swift leaped forward, but her foot slipped on a half-melted chunk of ice, and she fell face first on the pavement. Her mace slid just out of reach.

I raced toward them, jumping over her just in time to deflect a blow from the phoenix's clawed foot. It flapped its wings furiously, sending ice and water everywhere, blinding me.

"Dammit, Blackwell!" Swift shouted, dodging under the wing as she tried to get back to her mace.

I sliced through a feather and narrowly dodged a spray of blood. "Let's see you come up with a better idea! Just hitting it with your mace isn't actually *doing anything*," I yelled back.

I dodged left, but something hard hit the back of my knees and swept my legs out from underneath me. My back hit the pavement, and my katana clattered out of my hands. Swift looked down at me, half-apologetic, half-annoyed.

"Watch where you're going!" she said, exasperated.

"How about you watch where you're swinging that thing!" I snapped, rolling through the slush to grab my sword.

The asphalt rolled under our feet.

Swift looked at me, her eyes wide. This wasn't the phoenix. They could breathe fire and were nearly indestructible, but they did *not* cause earthquakes.

I grabbed my sword and ran after Swift. The asphalt cracked right under her feet, widening slowly. She leaped onto a car to avoid being swallowed up. This was all wrong.

Behind us, the ground split open, and green fire erupted from the crevice. It swallowed cars and a deluge of melted ice. Steam poured out like a fog as the cold water hit the hot air.

The phoenix fell halfway in and screamed, fire erupting from its beak. Its massive wings beat in a panic, sending debris and steam flying in every direction. Whatever was coming out of the earth was hotter than even the phoenix could stand.

Dark magic shuddered in the air all around us. Something, or someone, else was here.

"You feel that, right?"

Swift nodded, adjusting her grip on her mace and searching the area around us. She froze. "Who the hell is that?"

A cloaked figure stepped into view.

TWO

"**B**lessed be the sacrifices," a deep, grating voice boomed across the space. He lifted one hand, holding something I couldn't quite see from here.

I did know one thing, though. The magic that I felt pouring out of this guy had to be a warlock's magic. They were evil and power-hungry. Unsatisfied with the magic all mages were born with, they sought to gain even more, no matter the cost. If he was a warlock, our bad day was about to get worse.

The phoenix let out a shriek, flailing wildly as the fire consuming it suddenly blazed even higher. The bright feathers turned to ash, falling like snow on the wind that whipped around us.

A bright red light flew out of the phoenix and connected with whatever the warlock held. He cackled as the strange device glowed in his hand.

"What the hell is this guy's issue?" Swift muttered. "I'm all for roasting the phoenix, but I don't like where this is going."

"Me neither. I think he's a warlock, and I'm a little worried we might be the sacrifices."

"Should we stop him?" she asked, eyes still burning bright with berserker rage.

"Hey! You in the cloak!" I shouted over the noise. His head turned toward me slowly. "Are you about to kill us?"

His face was barely visible under the hood of his cloak, but I could still see the chilling smile I received in response to my question.

"Yeah, that's a warlock," I said uneasily. "We have to stop him. He's probably the one that summoned the phoenix in the first place."

"Let's go then," Swift said, charging in.

"Wait—"

It was too late. She raised her mace overhead with a battle cry.

I ran after her; there was no other option. The warlock lifted his other hand. Black and green fire poured from his palm. It twisted together and raced toward us. Lifting my katana, I invoked the shield rune at the same time that Swift swung her mace at the magical attack. All three hit simultaneously. A shockwave exploded outward, slinging us back like rag dolls.

I hit a car, my back shattering the window, and slid down into a heap on the ground. My vision swam and I couldn't hear anything other than my own heart pounding. I pushed up onto my knees, but a second blast wave hit me in the side, knocking me right back down as it tossed me further down the street.

There were people screaming behind me. The prosaic police had tried to get the area evacuated while we fought, and now they were running too. I couldn't blame them.

A whisper, dark and evil, passed through my mind, but I couldn't hear what it said. I shook my head, trying to clear it, and dragged myself back up to my feet.

This guy was pissing me off. I let go of everything I had been holding back. This city block was already toast, might as well destroy a little more of it and stop this warlock. Dark mayhem magic swirled around me, then raced toward him.

Releasing this much, this fast, was impossible for me to completely control. The magic lashed out as it flew towards him, ripping through a building the phoenix had already damaged and reducing it to rubble. I ground my teeth together and yanked the mayhem back toward the warlock.

A dark grin split his face, and he lifted up a strange golden amulet. The mayhem magic smashed into it and … didn't destroy it.

My eyes went wide as I felt the thing sucking my magic out of me. It stretched between us in a line of pitch black, twisting and rolling like a river. I fell to my knees, pain coursing through every nerve. It felt like I was being turned inside out. Or my soul was being ripped away from my body.

A shout cut through the roar of magic. Swift ran toward the warlock, wielding her mace. He swiped his hand at her, and a blast of green fire hit her like a battering ram.

"No!" I yelled, attempting to physically wrest control of my magic away from the warlock and the strange amulet, but my muscles wouldn't respond. My fingers twitched slightly as I struggled against whatever had me frozen in place.

Swift screamed under the onslaught of magic. It forced her backward along the asphalt. She lifted her palms and the familiar pink glow pushed back against the warlock's attack. A shield formed in her hand, deflecting the magic around her like a fiery river.

She looked at me, sweat dripping from her forehead, her teeth bared in a grimace. He was overpowering her. She couldn't hold him back for much longer.

I lifted my hand slowly. My limbs felt like they weighed hundreds of pounds. My fingers grasped at the magic flowing out of me, but the magic simply burned my fingers. I couldn't hold onto it.

My vision wavered and I fell to my knees. Swift tried to stand, but the warlock simply pushed a little harder and she faltered. Her shield cracked.

I struggled to breathe as my lungs spasmed in my chest. The amulet tore the magic from my very cells, leaving emptiness behind.

A blazing streak of white and gold shot over me, landing right in the stream of magic being sucked from my body.

A presence warmed me, easing some of the dizziness that had overtaken me. A snow-white leg appeared in the corner of my vision. I looked up as best I could and saw a giant fox at least four meters tall, with teeth as long as the blade of my katana. She advanced on the warlock.

It was Yui, the kitsune. Her coat was pure white, though her two tails were tipped in bright, fiery red.

With a low growl, she bit the stream of magic pouring out of me and wrenched her head from side to side, snapping it like a rope. The remaining magic rushed back into me, leaving me breathless from the impact.

"No!" the warlock bellowed, his voice cracking with rage. He abandoned his attack on Swift and thrust both hands toward the kitsune.

Yui jumped out of the way and turned toward me instead. For a brief moment, I thought she was about to eat me, but instead, she picked me up gently with her mouth and darted out of the way of another attack.

"We have to get Swift!" I shouted as she began to turn like she was about to just run away.

She huffed, hot breath blasting me in the face, but bounded toward my partner. Each jump rattled me painfully. I didn't have much to hold onto unless I wanted to cling to a tooth. It was already really slimy in her mouth, which I didn't want to think about.

I reached my arm down as the kitsune passed over Swift. She jumped up, grabbing my arm and almost pulling it out of its socket.

"This is not finished," the warlock shouted behind us.

Yui turned her head to face him, swinging us around. I almost lost my grip on Swift, but she managed to pull herself up to hang onto the kitsune's teeth.

"You will not consume the child I guard," Yui said. Her mouth didn't move, but her voice echoed all around us.

The warlock stepped closer and lifted the device. "I will consume *everything*," he growled.

The device flared to life and Yui shuddered. White magic drained from her for a moment, but she jerked away, snapping the connection.

Without waiting for another attack, she turned and ran.

THREE

"We have to stop him!" I shouted as Yui ran through the streets.

"*Thank you for saving my life. What would I do without you? You're so wonderful,*" Yui said, deepening her voice as she mocked me. "The warlock is already gone. Just be happy you're alive."

Yui slid to a stop a few blocks away and spat me out unceremoniously on the ground. I didn't quite manage to catch myself, but I did keep my skull from bouncing off the concrete.

Every muscle in my body ached. Even my bones hurt. Whatever that warlock had done to me wasn't good. I felt almost empty inside. A part of me was terrified I had no magic left.

Rolling onto my back, I grabbed the handle of my

katana, and the runes flared under my touch. I let my head fall back in relief.

Swift dropped nimbly to the ground beside me and extended a hand to help me up. I grasped it and let her pull me to my feet.

She immediately shoved me backward. "Are you kidding me with the ice? There was no way that was going to work!"

I shoved her right back, though she didn't move and my burned fingers stung from the impact. "It was better than continuing to do the same thing, which had already failed repeatedly!"

"I was wearing it out!" Swift objected, her eyes flashing in anger. Her trench coat was shredded, and she looked like she'd been rolling around in the mud.

Yui snorted behind us, her kitsune form melting into a woman dressed up like Chun-Li, the Street Fighter character. "Neither of you were doing anything effective against the phoenix or the warlock," she said, rolling her eyes.

"Were you watching us?" I asked, turning my frustration on her.

"Some of it," Yui acknowledged with a shrug.

I ground my teeth together in anger as I struggled to keep from shouting at her. "How did you stop that warlock? And why didn't you show up earlier if you could do all that?"

She scoffed. "I'm your guardian. I can only get involved when you're about to die."

"That's bullshit. Who makes up these rules?"

"I could tell you, but then I'd have to kill you. And I can't," Yui said smugly before turning into a fox and bounding away over the tops of abandoned cars.

"She is the worst," Swift muttered.

Sirens wailed in the distance as my phone rang in my pocket. I pulled it out and saw Bradley's name flashing on the screen. I jabbed my finger against the glass and answered the call.

"Blackwell," I bit out.

"You're alive. Does that mean that damn phoenix is dead?" he asked, not sounding nearly relieved enough to hear we had survived, in my opinion.

"Yeah, but that's not really good news," I said.

"Why the hell not?" Bradley demanded, his voice raising a few decibels.

"We found out who summoned it. We've got a warlock," I said, dread settling in my gut.

Warlocks were the mages' worst fear. Not only could they kill us, they also made us look bad. They were mages once, until they sold their souls for dark magic.

This was going to get worse before it got better.

FOUR

I winced as I watched a replay of the magic being sucked out of my body. When Swift and I had walked into Bradley's office he'd pointed at the chairs in front of his desk, then started this recording.

Bradley waited until Yui showed up, then paused the video. He sighed deeply, as though it had pained him to watch the disaster unfold.

He turned toward us, bracing his hands on the desk. He looked at Swift, then looked at me and shook his head. His mustache bristled with disappointment. "That was an embarrassment to the IMIB and to *me, personally*," he ground out. "You looked like a couple of buffoons out there! Novices! Tripping and working against each other! What do you have to say for yourselves?"

I glared at him, refusing to reply.

"Well, we were just...the phoenix was a lot more powerful than expected," Swift began, actually trying to explain away the clusterfuck that we had just gone through.

"And another thing!" Bradley shouted, cutting her off. "Why the hell did a kitsune show up to save your asses? Anyone care to explain?" He turned his glare on me and crossed his arms, waiting for a reply.

"Yui, the kitsune, has decided that since I returned her ball, she is my guardian," I said, still bitter about that even though she had saved my life. She kept eating all my Oreos. "I think a better question is, how did no one with the Mage's Guild see this warlock coming? They don't appear out of nowhere. There are usually signs."

Bradley scoffed. "There have been signs, but up until yesterday, the warlock was only active in Mexico and South America, not causing any real problems. They're still trying to figure out if this is even the same asshole."

I dragged my hand down my face. Communication was awful in the IMIB. If someone had just told us a warlock might have been involved, we could have been more cautious.

"We need all the information the IMIB and the Mage's Guild has on the warlock," Swift said, anger leaking into her voice. She was normally so proper with Bradley, but I guess this was too much even for her to stay calm.

"I'll see if I can get it," Bradley said, pushing off his desk and walking over to the screen. He hit rewind, playing the part where Swift slipped in the ice and ended up knocking me over with her mace again.

He paused it and turned back to us. "Fix this," he demanded, jabbing his thumb back at our faces, frozen in ridiculous expressions.

I slunk down in my chair. There was only one person...well, two, that could help us.

This was going to be miserable. I was too old to start training again.

"This is all your fault," I said, turning my glare on Swift.

She returned it, narrowing her pink eyes at me. "It's not my fault you're a klutz."

FIVE

As we walked out of Bradley's office, I tapped on Swift's elbow and nodded toward the elevators. A muscle in her jaw twitched like she might refuse and tell me to go jump off the Edge, but after a moment she nodded and followed.

Something Bradley had said bothered me. The Mage's Guild had known about the warlock but hadn't said anything until after he had attacked. They were notoriously bad at sharing information, but this was worse than usual.

We couldn't trust them to share what they knew, and I didn't want to talk about the case at the office where it was likely they were listening in. I didn't have proof our offices were bugged, but I wasn't going to risk it. I needed to contact someone special that could help us get what we needed, whether the Mage's Guild gave us the information willingly or not.

We rode the elevator down in silence. Tense, uncomfortable silence tinged with lingering frustration.

Swift and I were two of a kind. We liked to do things our way. Unfortunately, in a fight, that meant we stepped on each other's toes constantly. It was a lost cause, but I missed the days when I could just work alone.

As we rode the escalator down to level four for the Rune Rail to Tokyo, Swift looked at me, confused.

"Are you dragging me back to Tokyo for another overpriced dinner?" Swift asked, raising her brow.

"No, but I have some thoughts that are better discussed in a place I know is private," I said, stepping off the last step of the escalator and weaving through the crowd. According to the giant clock hanging from the ceiling, it was morning in Tokyo, so there was a big rush of people jamming onto the Rune Rail. I had completely lost track of time with the chaos of the last few hours. At this point, I wasn't even sure how long I'd been gone. It must have been twenty-four hours since I had last slept.

"Alright, but we're going to have to order in some food. I'm starving," Swift said, pressing her hand to her stomach, which growled loudly at the mention of dinner. Or breakfast. Or whatever meal this was.

"We're going to have to order a lot of food if Yui is there," I groaned. "I don't understand how she eats so much. It's like she's a black hole hell-bent on consuming all food in the universe."

Swift laughed. "I'm sure it's not that bad."

"You won't be saying that when she's stealing food right out of your hand," I grumbled, thinking back to the toast she had grabbed in her fox form right before I got to take a bite. She'd slipped under the couch and eaten it before I could catch her. Trickster my ass. She was just a *dick*.

"That reminds me," Swift said with a mischievous grin. "You lost the bet. I clearly saw you destroy that building, which means you have to keep Yui."

The magic that had bound the wager surged between us, making my palm itch. I glared at her, furious. I was getting sick of losing to her. "The phoenix did most of the damage," I muttered.

She laughed at me. "The magic agrees with me, loser."

The Rune Rail arrived, and Swift and I let the rush of people carry us on board. There was nowhere to sit, so we held onto the handrail for the short trip. I almost fell asleep just standing there, but we had to get one last thing settled before I crashed.

Luckily, the subway ride from the Rune Rail to my neighborhood was short. I put in an order to a local delivery place so that the food would show up a few minutes after we got to my apartment.

"Now that we're out of Moira," Swift said, startling me out of my thoughts as we walked down the street, "what is it that you wanted to discuss?"

"The Mage's Guild didn't warn IMIB about this warlock, which makes me think they're trying to hide his existence for some reason," I said with a shrug.

"I agree, and it worries me," Swift said. "We need to find out what they're hiding, and why."

I looked at her, surprised. We didn't normally agree. "Well, that makes this next part easier. I thought I'd have to talk you into investigating that."

"No," Swift said, raising her chin in determination. "No one can be above the law, especially not the Mage's Guild. If they saw this warlock coming and didn't try to stop him, then they're partially responsible for everything that happens."

I nodded at the doorman as he opened the door to the apartment building. "I know someone that can get us information, possibly even the real reason they hid the warlock."

"Who?" Swift asked. "They have their information systems locked down unbelievably tight."

"Nothing is unhackable," I replied with a grin.

Swift shook her head but followed me up to my

apartment. I pressed my hand against the rune that locked it down. It glowed, and the door unlocked.

Yui wasn't on the couch, or seemingly in the apartment at all. I let out a sigh of relief. "Thank the gods for that," I muttered, tossing my things on the small table by the door and stripping out of my suit jacket. It would have to be added to the pile of ruined clothes that kept growing, especially since meeting Swift.

"Toward the end of the fight, was that warlock draining your magic from you somehow?" Swift asked as she plopped down on my couch.

I rubbed my chest, which still ached slightly. "It felt that way," I admitted. "I could barely move, and I couldn't stop it at all."

"I've never seen anything like that, not even in all my years in Magical Artifacts," Swift said, worry creasing her brow. "Did you get a good look at what he was holding?"

I shook my head. "It looked like it was made of gold or something like it, but I couldn't see the design."

There was a brief knock at the door. I looked out the peephole to make sure it was the delivery person, then opened the door and accepted the food. "Thanks," I said perfunctorily, handing him a tip.

He nodded and hurried away.

"I got katsudon and curry rice. Take your pick," I

said, passing Swift the bag. "There's also a few other things in there, including some sushi."

Swift divvied up the food, scooting the curry rice toward the end of the coffee table. I opened the sushi and picked up a big piece with a slice of bright red tuna on top.

Halfway to my mouth, there was a pop, and orange flashed in front of me as teeth nicked my fingers. "Dammit, Yui! Stop doing that!" I shouted as the kitsune skidded around the shoji paper to hide in my room, the piece of sushi already chomped and gone.

SIX

The food was eaten. Yui was pouting behind the shoji divider because I had cast a shield to keep her from snatching anything else. And I was getting sleepy.

"Alright, it's time to talk to Bootstrap," I said around a yawn.

"Who?" Swift asked, yawning herself.

"He's a runehacker, and a computer hacker for that matter," I explained as I pulled out my laptop. I'd been given specific instructions on how to contact him the first time I hired him, which I followed carefully now. One mistake and he'd blacklist me. "I haven't needed his services in months. I try to avoid using him, honestly, but this is one situation where we need him."

"Runehacker? I thought that was a myth," Swift said, looking unconvinced.

I shrugged. "I thought so at first, but I've seen what he can do. Everyone says it's impossible, but he does it." I typed in the password, then hit enter. "Alright, now we just have to wait. It normally only takes him a few minutes to get back to me."

"This guy better be legit," Swift muttered.

"Don't let him hear you say that," I said, glancing at the screen nervously. "He can be a little touchy."

"I'm not touchy, asshat," a warped voice announced from the speakers on my laptop. "And tell Detective Alexis Antoinette Tiberius Swift not to question my mad skills."

"How did you–" Swift started, her jaw opening and shutting like a fish.

"Alexis...Tiberius...that's your full name?" I asked, barely holding back laughter.

Swift glared at me. "If you tell anyone I'll kill you," she threatened.

"Damn, she's kinda mean, Logan," Bootstrap said, his laughter crackling through the speakers.

"You have no idea," I muttered.

"What do you need? It's been a while since you hit me up," Bootstrap asked. "And it better be interesting, I'm kinda busy."

"We think the Mage's Guild tried to cover up the existence of a warlock—" I started.

"You mean the one that blew up part of New York

City this morning? He totally kicked your ass, dude," Bootstrap said with a chuckle.

"Thanks for that summary," I ground out. "Yes, that warlock. The Mage's Guild claims to have known he existed, but thought he was staying in Mexico. Since this is the first time the IMIB is hearing anything about him, that's crap."

"Since I'm already on it, just because I was curious and stuff, I'll give you a discount," Bootstrap said. "I'll send the routing and account info...now." My laptop pinged with the message. "Send twenty big ones, and I'll make sure you have the info in twenty-four hours."

"I'll have it to you in about ten minutes," I said, internally grimacing at the amount. It's a good thing my pockets were deep.

"Peace out, Logan. And tell that kitsune I said hi. She's hot," Bootstrap said before abruptly signing off.

"How does he know about..." Swift gestured toward Yui, staring at the laptop like he might still be listening. And...there was a good chance he was.

I shut the laptop. "Hell if I know. I stopped asking those questions around the second time I had to talk to the guy."

"Weird," Swift said, shaking her head. "And it only cost twenty bucks? I was expecting more."

I laughed. "Twenty thousand."

"Oh," Swift said, swallowing uncomfortably. "I would help, but..."

"Don't worry about it," I said, waving away her concern. "I wouldn't have contacted him if I couldn't cover it. I didn't expect you to pay half."

She was always so concerned about money. That still bothered me. She wasn't irresponsible, so there was no way she had blown her entire inheritance like some mages did. It was possible she had wasted it all on some charity project, but it didn't seem like that was the reason.

I might have to contact Bootstrap again for a little side project. Soon.

SEVEN

"Well, aren't you two cozy," Yui said loudly, intentionally waking us.

I forced one eye open and found myself looking through a curtain of pink hair. Sputtering, I brushed it away and sat up, my sore neck protesting the abrupt movement. Swift groaned and started to wake up. We had apparently fallen asleep on the couch, head to head. Thankfully, there wasn't cuddling involved or anything embarrassing like that.

Yui stood by the door, dressed casually in jeans and a blouse for once, with a half-eaten bag of my Oreos in her hand. "Late night?"

"And a long week, thanks to you," I muttered.

Yui shoved a whole cookie in her mouth and glared at me while she chewed.

"I'm going to run by my apartment and shower."

Swift stood and smoothed her hair down, or attempted to. It was creased from her odd sleeping position and didn't want to lay flat. She gave up with a grunt and brushed past Yui. "See you at the office in an hour and a half?" Swift looked over her shoulder to confirm, one hand on the doorknob.

I nodded. "Yeah, I don't want to wait for Bradley to send someone to drag us back to the IMIB."

Swift smirked and pulled the door open. "I'm sure today will be exciting."

"Don't say that," I groaned. "You've jinxed it."

She snorted and stepped outside. "Don't be so dramatic," she said before pulling the door shut behind her. The wards flared to life, re-engaging the magical protections.

Yui plopped down on the couch and got busy making *another* mess. I shook my head and retreated to the bathroom, taking a quick shower so I could have time for a proper breakfast. I wanted something hot. Something that Yui couldn't steal bites of.

I walked to my room, slipping behind the divider. Yui had turned on the TV and wasn't paying any attention to me, which was ideal.

"Your girlfriend is getting attacked," Yui said, sounding bored.

"I don't have a — wait, do you mean Swift?" I

demanded, pulling my pants on as fast as I could and grabbing a shirt as I ran out to the living room.

"Of course I mean Swift," Yui replied.

"How long? And how do you even know that?" I grabbed my katana and hurried to the front door, shoving my feet in my shoes.

Yui shrugged. "A few minutes, I guess. I figured I'd give her a chance to take care of it before I made a big deal about it, but one of the attackers has a massive magical signature. I'm surprised you can't sense it."

"Dammit, Yui."

I ran out of the apartment. I hadn't been truly mad at the kitsune before this. Eating all my food — especially my Oreos — and making a mess was annoying, but I could deal with it. Letting my partner get hurt was a whole different story. If Swift was injured, the kitsune would be finding a different place to wreck.

I jabbed the button for the elevator, but it was eight floors down already and headed in the opposite direction. Not willing to wait, I ran for the stairwell, slamming the door open. I jumped over the railing, dropping down to the level below me. I made it to the ground level floor in just a few seconds.

If it wasn't one thing, it was another. We'd barely had time to breathe after the last case before the warlock had attacked, and now this. She really shouldn't have destroyed whatever piece of shit magical weapon she stole.

As soon as I stepped out onto the street, the location of the fight became glaringly obvious. Magic lit up the sky barely a block away. Swift's magical signature over-powered the others, but I could sense the man Yui had mentioned. He felt dark, if not quite as powerful overall as Swift.

I sprinted down the street, dodging the prosaics that were walking quickly away from the fight. Fights between mages no longer freaked them out like it had in the beginning. They just turned and walked the other way, which was the smartest option. The scent of ozone made my nose tingle. Magic, especially offensive magic, stank of it.

An impact shook the street, setting off a car alarm, as I came around the corner. Swift was between two men, a redhead with a bushy beard and a guy as skinny as a toothpick.

Ginger had a fireball in each hand. He threw one at Swift, who turned around and hit it dead on with her mace. The magic sizzled and popped like a firecracker as it scattered. Toothpick darted in, arcane magic bursting from his palms in a shockwave that forced Swift back.

They continued dancing around each other, clashing in quick bursts, but there was a third assassin somewhere. I held back, trying to find him. What was he waiting on?

A whisper of magic tingled at my senses. I didn't like this. It felt like some kind of odd trap. Toothpick pushed Swift back farther. Every attack from both of them seemed to force her closer to the street.

Her foot slipped off the curb, and a fiery blast from Ginger shoved her back. A white hot rune flared under her and ropes shot up wrapping around her legs.

I cast a shield around her as I ran toward the fight. Less than a second after the shield surrounded her, a black streak of magic the size of a chopstick drilled into the side of it like some kind of magical arrow.

My eyes widened in horror. That's exactly what it was. There was a Spellsniper here.

Ginger turned toward me, teeth bared, and threw a fireball in my direction. I drew my katana and sliced it in half. He charged in like a bull, roaring his displeasure. I stepped to the side and kicked his legs out from under him.

Another arrow hit the shield Swift was trapped in, shattering it. She ducked, driving the handle of her mace down against the rune that had her trapped. Toothpick darted in, trying to catch her off guard with a quick strike, but she batted his attempt away.

I caught Ginger under the chin with a kick. He stumbled backward, and I drove my katana through his gut.

Normally, I would try to avoid any risk of killing him, but not today. Today I was done. Swift was pinned down, and these guys wanted her dead. There was no time for me to baby them.

Yanking the katana free in a spray of blood, Ginger collapsed in front of me. His hand clutched uselessly at his gut as he bled out. I charged toward Toothpick, who wasted no time slinging three fast blasts at me. I deflected the first two but had to jump out of the way of the third.

With a shout, Swift slammed her mace down a final time, shattering the rune that held her with brute force. She lunged forward as a magical arrow streaked overhead.

Toothpick ran to his left and threw an arcane strike past me. It caught Swift in the back, slamming her down onto the concrete sidewalk. Her chin bounced off the ground, but it barely phased her. She rolled with it and jumped back up to her feet.

"Come on, you coward!" Swift yelled, magic blazing around her like a whirlwind as she searched the tall buildings for the sniper. "Just fight me!"

The third assassin's magical energy was fading. He was giving up.

Toothpick drew our attention back with a particularly powerful attack that careened straight toward Swift. She hit the blast and forced it down onto the sidewalk. Chunks of concrete blew around her legs as it exploded.

She gritted her teeth and charged him. If she had been running at me like that, I'd have turned tail and fled. Toothpick, to his credit, stood his ground. I couldn't decide if he was brave or stupid. He thrust his palms out, intending to cast again, but he never got the chance. She swung her mace and magic flared out from the center. A ball of pink light hit him in the chest, blasting him across the street and into a wall. He hit with a loud crack, then fell to the ground, limp.

Swift stood in the street, her chest heaving with anger and exhaustion. The third guy was running away. Cowardly? Yes, but also smart.

"Are you okay?" I had to fight down the urge to drag her out of the street.

She snorted. "Just peachy."

I tightened my grip on my katana. "How many attempts is that now?"

Her mace vanished with a crack and she walked toward me. "It doesn't matter."

"Like hell it doesn't," I said, stepping into her path. "They're wearing you down, and they're getting smarter. Eventually, they're going to succeed or get lucky."

"Just butt out!" Swift shouted.

I ground my teeth together. "Why can't you just admit you need help?"

"This is my problem, no one else's. I'll deal with it." She squared her shoulders and jutted out her bloodied chin stubbornly.

"But you aren't dealing with it, and it's not going to just go away," I said, getting in her face. "No matter how many assassins you beat down, they'll send more."

"What am I supposed to do then, huh? Just give up?" Swift snapped. "I will *not* crawl back to my parents and beg for forgiveness. I did the right thing. They are *wrong*."

When I didn't reply, Swift turned on her heel and walked away.

I watched her go, limping slightly, but absolutely determined. They would kill her eventually. Another injustice made possible by wealth and status. I curled my fingers into my palm, deciding that I couldn't, and wouldn't, let that happen.

EIGHT

Sergeant Lopez rapped on the door frame before stepping through the open doorway of my office. She had on heeled boots that made her a few inches taller than usual, but she'd still only come up to my shoulder. Her dark brown hair was swept back in a ponytail. "Swift off today?"

"No, just running a little late this morning." I leaned back in my chair and ran my hands down my face, still mentally tired from the recent fights. "Did you need something?"

"The Big Chief told me to come volunteer to assist on the case. Something about you two being like water and oil?" Lopez leaned against Swift's desk with a smirk.

I gave her a sour look. "She doesn't listen. Ever. Just barges in swinging that mace like she's invincible."

Lopez snorted and raised a brow. "Sounds like someone else I know."

"Are you suggesting I do that?"

"You said it, not me," Lopez said, raising her hands in surrender.

Swift walked into the office, and my protest died on my lips. Her hair was still wet from a recent shower. "Hey, Lopez. Let me guess, Bradley sent you to help?"

Lopez nodded. "You two did kinda get your asses kicked."

Swift groaned. "Don't remind me. I hate phoenixes."

"It's the warlock that worries me," I said, standing and grabbing my tablet. The wall screen flicked on as I accessed the System and sent my search there.

The pictures from the surveillance videos showed a hooded figure. There wasn't a single clear picture of his face, just shadows and an occasional flash of glowing eyes. We already knew he was a magic user. Shifters, like Lopez, had eyes that would reflect light, but they didn't glow like a mage's. It was easy to tell the difference in a picture.

"He didn't come out of nowhere. A mage doesn't become a warlock overnight, and they sure as hell don't get that powerful without months, or even years, of work," I said.

"That amulet had to have come from somewhere as well." Swift walked over to look more closely at the photo. It was grainy and unfocused because of the magic. "The Mage's Guild and the IMIB have spent a lot of time and effort trying to round up things like that. In fact, that was my entire job before this. This was either stolen or bought off the black market," she said, tapping the gold device on the screen.

"When I watched the video, I found it odd that the warlock drew something from the phoenix and from Blackwell, but not from you," Lopez said, nodding toward Swift. "What exactly is he gathering? And why?"

"And did he get enough?" Swift added, turning back to face us.

Her words hung heavy in the air. No matter what came next, it wouldn't be good. Another attack like the phoenix would mean more dead prosaics. If the warlock had gotten what he needed, that could mean an attack against the Mage's Guild directly.

"We need to find this guy. Odds are he's still in New York City," I said, exchanging a glance with Swift. Bootstrap always worked fast, but I needed him to be even faster than normal this time.

Sergeant Danner appeared in the doorway. "Put on your big kid pants, boys and girls," he drawled. "There's a magical infestation in NYC, and it's wreaking havoc."

"What are you talking about?" Swift asked, her brows pinching together in confusion.

"Unicorns," Danner replied.

"Shit." I grabbed my katana and followed the others as we raced toward the elevators. Bradley was shouting at everyone left in the office to go and help us.

"Don't try to freeze them this time," Swift hissed in my ear as we crowded onto the too small elevator.

"Don't trip over your own feet," I snarked back.

"Whoever kills the most wins," Lopez said, her smiling face appearing at my shoulder. "Whoever kills the least buys dinner for everyone."

"Deal," I said, accepting the wager immediately.

Swift smirked and nodded as well. "Prepare to be poor, Blackwell."

NINE

I hated unicorns. They were mean, ugly, and could sniff out a virgin from a mile away.

That last part probably wasn't true, but they did prefer to eat the flesh of virgins.

This was a complete disaster. Of all the supernatural creatures, why'd it have to be them? A herd of unicorns meant at least fifty of the beasts. We'd need all the backup we could get.

Swift was with me in one car, Lopez and Danner in another. Danner had taken lead as we drove but, as we neared the attack, directions became unnecessary. The rainbows shooting through the sky were hard to miss.

Prosaics ran screaming down the streets. Unicorns had been a big disappointment for them years ago when supernaturals came out of the closet. They were not the beautiful bastions of innocence and purity everyone had thought.

A stray, crackling rainbow blasted past our car, ending in an explosion behind us. I swerved out of its path and slammed on the brakes. Swift opened her door and jumped out. A high-pitched whinny sent a cold chill down my spine as I followed after her.

The last time I'd had to fight a unicorn I was fourteen. Hiroji had been with me then, and lucky for us, there had only been one.

"Time to kick some ugly horse ass," Lopez shouted over her shoulder with a grin before dropping to her hands and knees. Black fur rolled over her as she shifted into a huge panther. She was twice the size of a normal cat and had fangs I did *not* want to get up close and personal with. She shook out her fur and padded forward, jumping on top of a car to wait.

The thunder of hooves shook the ground beneath us and echoed off the concrete. Danner stood in the middle of the street behind us, his deft fingers making short work of a set of runes. A barrier shot up, blocking the street.

"Keep an eye out for the warlock!" I shouted to the others as a couple more cars of agents screeched to a halt behind us. Sirens from the prosaic police sounded in the distance, but they'd keep back while we dealt with this mess.

Colorful lights blazed in front of the herd as they rounded the curve in the street. Their white coats were splattered with blood and gore. The biggest one ran in front. His thick, jagged horn was pitch black. He neighed loudly, his mouth frothing, and tipped his head down.

Swift summoned her mace. I drew my katana. Lopez tensed, her thick muscles rippling under her coat. The unicorns careened toward us, and a rainbow erupted from the horn of the leader.

These rainbows were not the friendly, pot-of-gold shortcuts that showed up after a good rainstorm. They were more like shiny laserbeams of death. Somehow their horns captured and condensed light into a devastating form. I didn't care *how* they did it. I just wished they wouldn't.

Danner raced forward with a shout, flames rushing ahead of him and crashing into the rainbow. He had fought in the Mage Wars that my parents had helped to end, and you could tell. He was ferocious and, frankly, terrifying. Flames raged around him in a whirlwind that struck out with a flick of his hand.

Swift ran around him and smashed her mace into the next unicorn. The metal head slammed the beast into the concrete. It went down with a snarl.

"One," she shouted. And the game was on.

I slid my hand along the back of my blade, drawing

out the mayhem magic down the length of it. This was how Master Hiko had taught me to use it in the beginning, as a literal focus. I could use it without wiping out everything around me this way.

The herd flowed around Danner as he fought the leader, drawing their attention. Lopez jumped down onto the back of one of them, her teeth sinking into its neck. She ripped a chunk free, and it fell beneath her, a spray of blood arcing through the air.

I charged in, heading toward three of the ugly bastards. One spotted me and lowered its head like a bull. A brilliant rush of colors blasted from its twisted horn. I cut through the first blast with a swipe of my sword and dove under the second, hitting the ground with a roll.

When I leaped back up to my feet, I thrust the katana forward, sinking into the unicorn's neck. Black blood leaked down the blade and was quickly consumed by the mayhem magic. I yanked it free and slashed the blade in the direction of the other two. The magic arced toward them like a whip and cut through their thick hide. They fell but kept thrashing, shooting rainbows in every direction like a freaking machine gun.

I grabbed the horn of the unicorn I'd just killed and, bracing my foot on its head, broke it off. With a shout, I threw it like a spear. It sunk into the chest of one of the thrashing unicorns and exploded, killing both of them. Black bits of bitchy horse flew in every direction.

I couldn't avoid getting splattered with the remnants, and their slick blood seeped through the material of my suit. This was getting thrown away as soon as I got home.

Danner's blockade was keeping them from moving past our position, but it had created another problem. The unicorns had us surrounded, surging in from every direction.

This wasn't a herd, it was *herds*, as in plural. This motherfucker had summoned more than one.

I hated warlocks.

"There are people trapped up here!" Swift's voice broke through the chaos.

"Danner, you good?" I shouted, taking a swipe at a unicorn running past me.

"I'm fucking great!" he replied as he roasted two unicorns charging him while standing on the corpse of their fallen leader. Lopez was running around him, taking down every unicorn he couldn't get to with apparent glee. Her muzzle was stained black with unicorn blood.

"On my way!" I yelled at Swift, running toward her position. If there were people trapped, we'd have to try to get them over the barrier, which wasn't going to be easy.

I could sense magic in every direction from other IMIB agents, but everyone was still so overwhelmed that backup couldn't get to us any more than we could get to them.

As I ran up behind her, Swift punted a unicorn so hard she actually launched it into the air. It crashed, upside down, on top of a taxi.

"Where are they?" I asked, sliding to a stop beside her.

"Pizza Bob's," she said, slightly out of breath. "How many are you up to?"

"Three. You?"

"Five," she said with a vicious grin.

A high-pitched scream, followed by a crash, emanated from the pizza place in front of us. We ran toward the restaurant, almost bumping into each other as we both tried to take the same route around a pile of rubble. Grinding my teeth together, I jumped over it, just barely keeping from tripping when I landed.

A unicorn shoved its head through the plate glass window, and a blaze of color reflected on the shattered glass as it attacked whoever was in the store. An old metal trash can hit it upside the head, scattering the contents all over the sidewalk. While I appreciated the metaphor, tossing trash at it was not an effective way to stay alive.

Swift and I charged forward at the same time, and

the handle of her mace caught me in the gut as she swung it around.

"Watch where you're swinging that—"

A unicorn came out of nowhere and slammed into my side.

Lucky for me, this particular inbred demon horse had a horn that bent a little to the left. Instead of goring me, the point of the horn simply gouged a long line of flesh from my side to my back.

I drew my katana and thrust it backward, stabbing it into the creature's neck as we smashed into the brick wall of the pizza place. The resulting screech nearly split my eardrums. I stabbed it twice more, mostly out of anger, then shoved its dead body away from me.

"Four," I muttered. Blood was pouring out of my wound and it hurt like hell. That horn probably wasn't very sanitary, either. I was going to have to see an actual healer for this crap.

"What the hell are you doing back there?" Swift demanded as she fended off two more of the beasts.

"You clobbered me with your stupid mace!" I shouted angrily.

She faltered and finally looked back. Her eyes went wide when she saw that I was wounded.

Two people stumbled out of the broken window. The guy yelled, "Look out!"

I realized two things in the same instant. One, that

guy was Billy. I'd never seen him out from behind the Rune Rental desk, and almost didn't recognize him. Two, Swift was being gored by a charging unicorn she hadn't seen coming. *Shit.*

She was lifted from her feet as the horn sunk into her gut. Billy grabbed the girl next to him and pushed her to the ground, covering her as a second unicorn ran right over them. I beheaded it with one powerful swipe of my katana. The motion made the muscles on the left side of my body burn painfully, but I couldn't stop now.

Swift grabbed the unicorn's head with one hand, then punched it with the other. The first blow cracked its skull, and the second caved it in.

As it fell, I caught her and unceremoniously ripped her free. She screamed in pain, and really, I couldn't blame her. That had to hurt. Her eyes rolled back in her head, and she slumped in my arms, only half conscious.

There were at least a dozen more unicorns headed toward us, and with Swift hurt and Billy and the girl to think about, I couldn't stick around to kill them.

"Get up, we have to go!" I shouted, slipping my hands under Swift's legs to pick her up. She was heavier than I expected. I turned to retreat, but there were more unicorns headed from that direction. "Shit. Into the store!"

"Wait!" Billy shouted, running toward us. He laid his

hands on Swift's stomach, and light poured from his hands, wrapping around her torso. She jolted awake as the blood was sucked back into her body and the wound closed. Her stomach was smooth, as if it had never happened.

I dropped her feet and she shoved away from me, panting. Without hesitating, she summoned her mace once again.

"I'm gonna kill every last one of these stupid little ponies," she growled as she turned to face the charging beasts.

"Where the hell did you learn that?" I asked as Billy put his hands on my back around the cut.

"I'm going to college to become a Healer," he said, eyes darting to the charging unicorns.

The girl was huddled behind him and had a death grip on his bicep. I didn't recognize her, but I was guessing she had to be his girlfriend or something. He was a little beat up from the trampling he'd just received, but the worst of his injuries were just bruises.

Swift swung her mace down onto the asphalt and it rippled out in a wave, knocking down the biggest group.

Billy's healing magic seared through me, and I came alive like I'd just downed six energy drinks. No wonder Swift had snapped awake like that.

"You two should get back in the store for now, but be

ready to run," I said, preparing a spell in my free hand. They needed to be out of the way until we killed these bastards.

Of all the creatures that needed to go extinct, unicorns were at the top of the list.

TEN

"Nineteen. I beat you." Swift said, crossing her arms.

"No, we *tied*," I said, mirroring her posture. She had not beaten me. In fact, considering I'd sort of saved her life, I considered this my win.

Lopez snorted. "Well, I killed thirty."

I dropped my arms and protested, "Danner was helping you."

"He killed forty-five on his own," she said with a shrug. "You two idiots were the only ones that got injured, and you killed way less than everyone else."

Danner nodded in acknowledgment and flicked his toothpick on the ground. "I want barbecue."

Lopez grinned at that. "Meat sounds good right about now."

The contest had seemed like a good idea when I

thought I'd come out on top; now it was just humiliating. I glared at Swift. I used to win things before she showed up. She was my *unlucky* charm.

Billy waved at me with a smile, and I turned away from the group to walk towards him. He had one arm slung around the pretty blonde girl he'd been protecting from the unicorns. He said something to her, and she looked at me, then nodded. Getting up, he jogged toward me.

"That was *awesome*," he said, still practically vibrating with adrenaline.

I was covered in unicorn gore, smelled like rotten eggs, and every muscle in my body ached. "Awesome is not the word I'd choose, but glad you had fun. What were you even doing here? I didn't think you lived in New York."

"Oh, I don't," he said, glancing back at the girl. "I was just...well, Sarah said she liked pizza, and Jonas in billing said that this pizza place was the best, so I thought she'd like it." A blush crept up his neck and onto his cheeks.

"So, she's your girlfriend?"

The blush deepened. "I haven't asked her out."

I clapped my hand on his shoulder. "Billy, man to man, now is the time. You just threw yourself over her to protect her from the trampling hooves of a unicorn. You are her hero. It would almost be insulting if you didn't ask her out now. I guarantee she's expecting it."

"How do I even do it?" he asked, his voice cracking like a pubescent teenager.

"You walk up to her and tell her the next date you take her on will be way less life or death, then ask if she's free tomorrow night."

"That's it?" he asked, looking back at her again like he was afraid she might disappear at any moment.

"Yep. You can also kiss her, if she seems okay with it," I said, sticking my finger in his face. "She's just been traumatized, so it could go either way. But kissing is a very clear signal that you don't want to be friends." I spun him around and shoved him back toward the girl. "Go get her, tiger."

"Thanks, Blackwell," he said with a terrified expression. He marched toward the girl as though he were going to his doom.

Swift appeared at my shoulder. "What, exactly, did you tell him?"

"To man up and ask her out."

"Seriously?"

I shrugged. "He should find out if she's interested before he wastes a bunch of time pining after her."

Billy stopped in front of Sarah, and she stepped in close. That was a good sign. I couldn't hear them from where we were standing, but it was obvious from his mannerisms that he was currently stumbling over his words trying to ask her out.

She laughed, grabbed him by the head, and planted a kiss on his lips. He froze, arms hovering awkwardly to the side like a starfish. Finally, he wrapped them around her in a proper embrace.

"Sweet, isn't it?" Swift said, a blood-streaked smile on her face.

I snorted. "Sickeningly sweet."

"Are you backing out of buying us dinner, Blackwell?" Lopez shouted from behind us.

"I didn't lose! Swift and I *both* did," I shouted back.

"Whatever, I'm hungry! Let's go!" she said impatiently.

With one last glance at the two lovebirds, I followed Swift back to the car. At least somebody was having a good day.

ELEVEN

We'd gorged on barbecue until my wallet was significantly lighter and my belly so stuffed I could hardly move. Maybe that was why I couldn't sleep.

I had tried. I really had, but I couldn't get comfortable, and my brain wouldn't shut off. I swept the covers away and swung my legs over the edge of the futon, only to hit fur.

Yui yelped and jerked away, then snarled at me sleepily.

"Oh, shut up." I threw a pillow at her and stood. She huffed but curled up on the pillow, content. For now, at least. "Do not get in my bed," I warned as I shuffled out to the living area.

The wall screen flared to life as I grabbed my tablet, illuminating the room in a wash of blue. This was going to take another chunk of my bank account, but it should be worth it.

Following each step of the memorized instructions, I contacted Bootstrap for the second time in twenty four hours, then leaned back into the couch to wait.

And wait. And wait.

It had been at least five minutes already. I sighed and adjusted so I could lay my head against the back of the couch. As my eyes slipped shut, I heard a chuckle.

"You're not exactly Sleeping Beauty, dude," Bootstrap said.

"You, however, might be a fairy-tale villain." I opened my eyes, squinting into the glare of my screen. "Anyhow, I was contacting you about—"

"Swift? I know. I figured you'd be calling soon, so I already have the information ready," Bootstrap said, his chair creaking in the background.

"How did you know I'd be calling about Swift?" I asked, growing even more suspicious he had bugged my apartment somehow.

"She's your partner, and you didn't even know her real name. I was also curious about her, because — let's be real — she's banging, and the info I found blew my mind. This is some real Hamlet shit, dude. There's no way you knew all this already, and you hate not knowing things," Bootstrap said. I could practically hear the smirk through the connection.

"Since you already did the work to satisfy your own curiosity, does that mean I get a discount?"

"Hell no. You've already gotten one. Don't get greedy, man."

I scoffed in irritation, but I was actually pleased. *Finally*, someone was ready to offer me answers. He could have however much money he wanted. Knowledge was priceless. "Fine, what can you tell me?"

He clapped his hands together. "Where to start," he murmured absently. "Okay. Six months ago, she stole the Sigil of Unfettered Suffering from a magister's office."

With a groan, I ran my hands down my face. When she said she had stolen something, I had assumed she meant something unimportant. Some weapon that was too cruel to be used, but not anything worth dying over.

Of course, it was more than that. "She's insane."

Bootstrap chuckled. "Just wait, it gets worse. That magister was her uncle, and he got his ass handed to him for embarrassing the Mage's Guild. Swift, since she is one of *The Swifts*, was handed down a light sentence, which included being dismissed from her old job and a fine that makes my prices look budget friendly. She has a few weeks left to pay the fine, but...drum roll please...she hasn't done it yet. And can't."

"Why not? Her trust fund should be huge."

"Now, this took quite a bit of digging to figure out,

so, you're welcome," Bootstrap said smugly. "Turns out her parents froze her accounts. All of them. She is completely cut off. From what I can tell, they want her to come crawling back with an apology and start behaving like a proper Swift instead of doing grunt work for the IMIB. They have a position lined up for her and everything. Shockingly, she refused. They started sending the assassins about a week before she got partnered with you, presumably to intimidate her into complying, but boy, was that a dumb strategy."

I put my head in my hands. "They guaranteed she'd never comply when they did that."

"I have footage of the first attack, and *damn*, she is scary hot."

I leaned back with a sigh. "What happens if she doesn't pay the fine in time?"

Bootstrap whistled. "It's not good. Something like fifty years in Purgatory."

Purgatory was every mage's nightmare. It was the result of a warlock's spell gone wrong that the Mage's Guild had immediately put to use. It was a prison that fed off a mage's magic. Not enough to kill you, just enough to keep you weak, and probably drive you insane. Fifty years in a place like that was enough to break anyone, even Swift.

Bootstrap tapped his fingers against something, then sighed. "I can practically hear you thinking."

My nails bit into my palms. I was right when I'd told her that no one else could deal with her issues. Most days, I wasn't sure I wanted to either, but I couldn't let them take away her life for doing the right thing. Not when I had the means to stop it.

"How much is the fine?"

"It would be fifty-three percent of your net holdings...if you liquidated most of your assets," Bootstrap said, his tone more serious than I'd ever heard before.

The amount was almost too much to process. I pushed off the couch and paced the length of the living room. "Including the estate?"

"Yeah, man. Sorry."

"Don't apologize. It's just a house. It doesn't matter," I said, though I knew the anger in my tone suggested otherwise.

No wonder she hadn't asked for help. The fine was insane. It was borderline unpayable, and was most likely meant to be.

I hated the Mage's Guild.

TWELVE

S wift leaned back in her chair, twirling a pencil between two fingers. We had been poring over all the information the Mage's Guild had sent us concerning the warlock. Most of it was crap.

Swift yawned and dropped her feet to the ground. "Have you talked to Bootstrap again?"

"What?" I asked, feeling like I'd been caught for a moment.

"About the warlock," Swift said slowly, like I was stupid.

"No, I'd have told you." I stretched my arms overhead, then stood. Ever since finding out the complete truth about Swift's predicament, I had been restless.

"How's your side?"

I snorted. "Healed. How's your stomach?"

She put her hand over the spot the unicorn had gored her. "Also healed, but—"

Laughter erupted from outside the office.

"What the hell is going on?" I walked over to the doorway. The main screen, normally used for announcements, was playing a loop of me and Swift's recent...mishaps.

Swift walked out of the office and stopped dead in her tracks when she saw it. "You have got to be kidding me."

"If we try to avoid it, it'll only get worse," I said, clapping her on the shoulder before strolling toward the pranksters.

Danner was leaning against his desk, gnawing on a toothpick with a smirk. The video looped to my unfortunate goring, and his smirk grew into an actual smile. "It was even more hilarious in person," he said to the small group of IMIB agents gathered in front of the screen. One of them had popcorn.

Lopez was laughing so hard she could barely take a breath, her face bright red and her eyes wet with tears.

"I see you idiots have the latest blockbuster comedy," I drawled, getting their attention.

Sergeant Zhang turned around and grinned at me. "If it isn't the shish kabob himself. And his partner. Other shish kabob."

"You only wish you could look that badass getting

gored by a demented horse," Swift scoffed, gesturing at the screen as the unicorn sunk its horn into her gut. The clip ended with her beating its head in with her bare hands.

Zhang shrugged and tossed some popcorn in his mouth. "You kind of have a point."

Detective Peterson stood up in the front. He walked over to me, his chest puffed out. He was thrilled to see them making fun of me for once instead of him. "You're the worst agents in the whole IMIB. I'm surprised Bradley didn't fire you."

"Peterson, I see you're as stupid as ever," I said drily. At least he wasn't spilling coffee all over me today. Though him talking was almost as bad.

He scoffed, his lips twisted in a sneer. "You're the one that looked stupid when you were flailing around fighting ponies with horns."

Swift got in between us, forcing Peterson to take a few steps back. "Like you could have done better. You were the only agent that didn't show up to help."

Lopez scrambled to her feet and grabbed Swift's elbow. I was absolutely going to let Swift beat Peterson up, but it was probably good someone was being mature about it.

"Shut that off, losers," Lopez said, dragging Swift back toward our office.

I winked at Peterson, then followed.

Lopez shoved Swift into the office ahead of her. "You have a temper even worse than mine. You know Peterson is just an idiot, right?"

Swift sighed. "I don't like him. He's a coward."

"No one likes him," I said, strolling over to my desk and grabbing one of the files I had already read five times. Maybe if I read it again, something new would jump out at me. Some connection.

"In all seriousness though, you two need to sort out whatever it is that keeps making you trip over each other," Lopez said, crossing her arms and pinning Swift with what I could only describe as a *look*. All the softness was gone from Lopez's face.

"We're working on it," I said, saving Swift from needing to respond.

And we were. Sort of. I had a plan to, at least.

"Yeah, make sure you do," Lopez said, shaking her head as she turned to leave the office. "But if you keep screwing up, make sure it's recorded for our entertainment."

Swift groaned and plopped down on her desk, resting her head on her arms.

Waiting a few seconds for Lopez to get out of hearing distance, I cleared my throat and asked, "You were going to say something before we were interrupted?"

"It wasn't important," Swift said, waving a hand at me absently. That was most likely a lie.

"Just spit it out," I said. It wasn't like her to hesitate over what to say. She was almost as blunt as I was.

"We can't keep tripping over each other like this," she said, lifting her head. "I feel like a novice when I'm out there with you. It's going to get one of us, or one of our teammates, killed. They can mock us all they want, but it's a real problem." She pressed her lips into a thin line and looked at me, most likely waiting for me to blow up.

I sat on the edge of my desk. "I agree."

"Really?" she asked, raising her brow.

"Yes. In fact, I had been considering taking you to my old Master so that we could both get some training. Hiroji...well, we used to be unstoppable when we were still friends. Master Hiko taught us how to work as a team. Play to our strengths. Apparently, I forgot all that as soon as I met you."

"We can't spend months training. The next attack could be today. Hell, it could be in an hour," Swift said.

"I know, but we can spend the time when we aren't investigating the warlock, or getting our asses kicked, in training. Are you up for it?" I crossed my arms.

"Yeah, I guess I am," Swift said, despite still looking a bit hesitant. "Are you sure he'll be willing to teach us out of the blue like this? I've never even met him."

I laughed. "He'd never pass up an opportunity to give me a beating. Don't worry, he'll love you. In fact, he'll probably enjoy watching *you* beat me up." My smirk faded to a frown. Maybe I hadn't thought this through completely.

Swift's demeanor immediately changed as well. "Sounds great, when can we start? Until Bootstrap gets back to us, this whole investigation is pretty much stalled."

"There's something I have to do tomorrow morning, possibly into the afternoon. If you can be at my apartment at 2 p.m. Tokyo time, I'll take you to Master Hiko's place."

"What do you have to do?" Swift asked, looking surprised that I might have a life outside of my job.

"It's personal. Don't worry about it," I said, cutting off that line of questioning.

THIRTEEN

"Mr. Blackwell," the woman said, looking over the glasses perched on the end of her nose. She didn't seem to like what she saw. "This is highly irregular."

"Irregular, or not, it is well within my rights to settle this debt," I replied, handing her the third document that Bootstrap had sent with me. There was a lot of paperwork involved, none of which I understood, but he had assured me it was all in order. Apparently, a few lawyers owed him big, and they'd had the forms ready in a matter of hours.

Arbiter Laurent snatched the paper from my hand and looked it over carefully, her brow creasing a little more with each line she read. I resisted the urge to tap my foot impatiently, but only barely.

She lowered the paper and pinned me down with a

look. "If I file this, there is no going back. Do you understand? The money *will* be collected from your accounts."

I nodded. "Understood."

She laid the paper on her desk and began drawing a series of runes. Her fingers were nimble, dragging the bright orange magic through the air almost faster than I could track. The runes glowed and sank into the form. Lines of magic illuminated her desk like the threads of a spider web.

"That is all for my part. Please proceed to the drawing room to await the next step," she said, clasping her hands together in front of her tweed skirt.

I stood and nodded. "Thank you."

Halfway to the door she spoke again. "Mr. Blackwell."

I turned back, but she hesitated, clearing her throat uncomfortably. "Your parents would have been proud of this decision."

My breath caught in my chest, and my heart squeezed painfully. "You knew my family?"

She smiled tightly. "Yes. And you, when you were a child."

I swallowed, looking at the ground to hold back emotions I hadn't felt in a very long time. The pain of my parents' death had never left, but it was like an old wound that only ached when it was twisted. "Thank you."

"Just...be careful, alright? They would have wanted you safe as well," she said quietly. She cleared her throat and seemed to shake off the worry. "Hurry along now, it wouldn't do to keep the Lord High Chancellor waiting."

"He's the one I'll be seeing?" I asked, surprised.

"Of course, he requested to be alerted if there was any movement on this case," she said, her eyes boring into me.

I nodded, grateful in too many ways to count. "I hope to see you again, Arbiter Laurent."

"Likewise," she said with a nod.

The hallway was well lit, but oppressive nonetheless. The plush carpet muted the sounds of an otherwise bustling building. My mind whirred with all the new information. I was about to have a face-to-face meeting with the Lord High Chancellor, the second most powerful man in the world. Some would argue the *most* powerful, but never where they could be heard.

It was a pity I couldn't sock him across the jaw, but that wasn't worth dying over. Swift was crazy strong, but her father...he was something else. He had given berserker mages their reputation for being unstoppable.

The drawing room was empty save for a liquor cart, two stuffed chairs, and the most uncomfortable looking couch I'd ever seen. I made a beeline for the liquor cart and picked up a bottle of amber colored liquid.

The glass stopper pulled free without a sound. I gave

it a sniff. Scotch. Probably from a batch older than me. I flipped over a crystal glass and poured a finger, shrugged, then doubled it. Without bothering to try and enjoy it, I swallowed it down like a shot.

"That seems a bit wasteful," a man said behind me.

I turned to face the Lord High Chancellor. He was about my height and looked like he was in his late fifties, but he was at least five hundred years old. His gray suit was impeccable, and his jet black hair was only marred by the streaks of silver at the temple. The weight of his magical signature made my knees shake.

Putting the stopper back in, I shrugged. "If it's never drunk, it's more of a waste. How long has this been sitting in here untouched?"

The chancellor chuckled. "Probably for years. Most people don't dare pour themselves a glass." He walked farther into the room, stopping behind one of the chairs. "You, however, dare."

"I think the money I just transferred into the guild's coffers will cover a few drinks. Besides, that's pretty much my life motto," I said with a shrug.

"That is quite obvious," the chancellor replied, his fingers flexing almost as though he were resisting the urge to curl them into a fist. "Tell me, how exactly did my daughter talk you into paying off her debt? Based on my surveillance, I don't think the two of you are madly in love or anything similarly banal."

That was a question I didn't care to answer, but I had a sense I might not be leaving this room until I did. "The assassination attempts were getting annoying. Maybe I just wanted them to stop," I offered, knowing he wouldn't accept that explanation.

These games of trying to trap a person with their words weren't exactly my thing. I was hesitant to tell him too much. Anything could – and likely would – be used against me later, and I had no idea how.

The chancellor scoffed at my weak lie. "Don't skirt around the truth; it isn't your style. Be daring, Blackwell."

This was a bad idea, but I was the King of Bad Ideas. "The decision of the Mage's Guild was wrong. You cutting her off so that she couldn't pay the fine was worse. I couldn't stand by and allow an injustice like that to occur without doing something."

The chancellor smiled at me as though I were an unruly child. "You sound just like your parents," he said, making it clear that was not a compliment.

"I've been hearing a lot about my parents lately."

"Odd how that happens, isn't it? Reminders of things you'd hadn't thought about in years have a tendency to show up in unexpected ways," the chancellor commented as he took a step toward me. "However, it's completely unimportant in your current situation." He lifted his hand and I was slammed back into the wall. I hadn't even felt the spell spark in the air. It had been instantaneous.

He prowled forward while I struggled to breathe, pinned like a bug against the wooden panels. His eyes glowed deep red as if he were a demon. "If you interfere with my plans for my daughter *ever again*, I will put you through such hell that you will beg for death. Do you understand?"

I ground my teeth together, fighting for the ability to speak. "Yes," I choked out. What I didn't say was that his threat wouldn't stop me. But I definitely understood.

He must have seen it, but he didn't kill me then and there. Instead, he turned and walked away. When I could no longer hear his footsteps, the pressure stopped, and I fell to the floor, panting.

That was one scary asshole. If I ever had to fight him, I would have to make the first strike, and it would have to be devastating.

FOURTEEN

I walked up to the house, Swift trailing behind me, with a growing feeling that this was a terrible mistake. Working with Swift was hard enough on a good day. Having to do it under Master Hiko's instruction was going to be tortuous. He didn't have any patience for excuses, and that was all I had right now.

As I raised my hand to knock, Sakura opened the door.

She pursed her lips and looked me over, then glanced at Swift. "This is not what I meant by visiting more often, but it will do. Is this your girlfriend that my Seijuro was telling me about?"

"Girlfriend? What? No!"

Sakura smiled as I became flustered and stepped back, inviting us inside. "You have always been so easy to rile up. It's why you could never succeed in my training."

"What branch of magic do you teach?" Swift asked curiously, no doubt eager to hear all about what I failed at.

I stopped Swift and pointed at her boots. She took a step back and quickly kicked them off, setting them next to mine on the shoe rack near the door. We then hurried to catch up to Sakura.

"Ninjutsu. It is a calm, focused magical art. Logan is chaos personified." Sakura paused, looking back at Swift critically. "You are not much better. Berserker mage?"

"Yes," Swift replied, looking shocked.

Sakura shook her head. "All the young ones seem to lack focus. Too much passion, too little sense."

She rounded the curve in the hallway ahead of us. Less than a second later we did as well, but she was already gone. A short way down the hallway, two doors stood open, leading into opposite rooms.

"Those are our rooms," I said, pointing at them.

Swift turned in a circle, looking all around and above us. "Where did she go?"

"No clue. I've never been able to figure it out."

I took the left room, while Swift took the one on the right. The guest rooms were simple. A futon, a low desk with a pillow, and a private bathroom that contained a tub.

This had been my room growing up. Swift was in the room Hiroji had occupied. I was sure Sakura had done it on purpose, probably to remind me what it had felt like to have a friend. A brother. Hearing Swift shuffle around in the room opposite mine gave me overwhelming feelings of nostalgia and regret.

I stripped out of my suit, feeling a little like I was shedding a persona, and changed into my training clothes. It had been well over a year since I had last worn them. The material smelled slightly musty from sitting in a drawer.

"You ready, or are you still primping?" Swift called from the hallway.

I opened the door to my room and flashed her a smile. "It takes a lot of work to look this good."

She rolled her eyes. "Where do we go?" Unlike my traditional uniform, Swift wore colorful leggings and a tank top the same shade of pink as her hair.

"This way," I said, leading her through the house toward the back door.

The path to the dojo led through the gardens. Master Hiko spent his free time maintaining them. He had told me that time with his hands in the earth creating something beautiful balanced his mind. Creation versus destruction.

It was late spring, so the garden wasn't at its peak,

but he managed to coax life and beauty from it throughout every season.

Swift walked slowly beside me, taking it all in with awe. "This is beautiful."

"I hated it when I first came here because Master Hiko made me pull weeds every day," I said, remembering the agony of being forced to sit outside under a hot sun after being spoiled by my parents my entire life. They had sent me to Master Hiko for training, and I had thought it was the worst thing that could ever happen to me — until my parents were killed. The garden became my refuge after that.

We stepped into the cool shade of the dojo, slipping our *uwabaki* — indoor slippers — off by the door, and walked inside. Master Hiko wasn't here, and knowing him, there was no telling when he'd actually show.

"How about a sparring match? Just to get warmed up," I offered.

"You warm up with sparring matches?" Swift asked, raising a brow.

I shrugged. "Sure, why not? You aren't scared, are you? I promise not to break your face this time."

"I *let* you hit me. Or did you not realize that?"

"It's hard to really tell something like that in a fight where we were both holding back."

"Can I assume no magic?" Swift asked.

"Correct." I shifted into a fighting stance, my hands

raised by my face. I rarely fought without my katana, but hand-to-hand was just as important a skill.

The glow in Swift's eyes dulled as she tamped down on her magic completely. She lifted her hands as well, and we circled each other. Impatient as ever, she threw the first punch. Her fist was lightning fast even without magical help.

I deflected the blow, countering with two fast strikes of my own. She slapped them to the side, dancing out of my way and forcing me to duck under an elbow strike, only to catch me in the side with a kick.

Master Hiko appeared in the doorway and we stepped apart, panting.

"From what you have told me, I already know you can fight each other. Perhaps we should test how poorly you work together?" Master Hiko said as he walked toward us.

"How are we supposed to test that?" I asked.

Master Hiko put one hand behind his back and lifted the other, motioning for us to attack him. "Fight me. I will even give you the advantage of four arms against one."

This was going to hurt, I just knew it.

"Don't charge in," I whispered to Swift.

"Don't hold back," she countered.

We moved around Master Hiko until he stood

between us, waiting for our attack. I waited for Swift to move first, as I knew she would.

She went for a straightforward attack, most likely meant to test his defenses. That was her first mistake. Her fist never made it anywhere near him. He stuck his foot out sideways and she ran straight into it. I could hear her wheeze from where I was.

I feinted left, then threw a hook punch, which Hiko simply ducked underneath. A punch caught me in the temple, but I wasn't sure which hand threw it. He followed up with a kick to my chest that knocked every last bit of air from my lungs and sent me stumbling backward.

"What a terrible start," Hiko scoffed.

Swift lunged for him, and he caught her with the same kick, harder this time. She flew back, hitting the wall with a thud. I came in with a kick. Hiko blocked with his shin and backhanded me. I mostly deflected the strike, but I couldn't stop the kick he threw along with it.

He didn't wait for either of us to recover this time. A flurry of punches and kicks rained down on me. I blocked and parried what I could, but more made it through my defenses than not.

Swift kept charging in and getting immediately thrown back. We had no strategy and no synergy. We were just two people getting beat up by the same one-armed man. The problem was, I had no idea how to fix it.

"Try something different, dammit!" I shouted at Swift.

She ran *around* Hiko instead of into him and forced herself in front of me. She managed to deflect a few strikes, but I couldn't help. Every direction I moved, Hiko managed to direct her as well, keeping me trapped outside of the action.

"Different is not always better," Hiko said, sounding bored. With a blindingly quick movement, he jumped and thrust both his feet into Swift's chest.

She flew backward, hitting me despite my attempt to dodge, and we fell to the ground. Bloodied. Bruised. And demoralized.

"Tch," Hiko scoffed. "Pathetic."

Swift rolled off of me with a groan. "I haven't gotten a beating like that since I was ten."

"It's only going to get worse. I'm pretty sure he was going easy on us," I said.

"Why are you laying around? Get up, this fight is not finished," Hiko said, interrupting our pity party.

I was right. This had been a *terrible* idea.

FIFTEEN

I slipped into the hot water and closed my eyes, resting my head on the stone edge of the hot spring.

"Keep your eyes shut," Swift hissed.

"No promises," I replied, despite having every intention to keep them screwed firmly shut. The last thing I needed was the sight of my partner's nude body seared into my memory.

"Blackwell, I swear—"

"I'm not going to peek. Just get in," I said, lifting my hand from the water and covered my eyes, motioning in her general direction for her to get in, then turned around to give her complete privacy.

"I still don't see why you have to be naked to get in a hot tub," she muttered.

I laughed. "It's an *onsen*. And that's just how it is. Some people call it *hadaka no tsukiai*, which basically means naked friendship. There are no formalities, no barriers. And the older generation sees it as dirtying the bath, which is extremely rude. Sakura is very traditional in some ways."

"Still not a fan," she said with a sigh. The hot water splashed as she stepped in, lowering herself into the *onsen* across from me with a pained hiss. "I know this is supposed to make it better, but *ow.*"

"Once you get used to the temperature, it feels amazing," I said, laughing at her slightly. Which was a mistake. Laughter hurt. My ribs hurt. Hell, even breathing was a little uncomfortable. "Is it safe to open my eyes?"

"Yeah."

It was dark outside; the moon was barely a crescent today. I could just make out her features, and from this far away, her modesty, and mine, was intact.

She slipped down until her chin was touching the water and plopped her slightly wet towel on top of her head. It hung unevenly down over one ear. "Did you grow up here or something?"

I shrugged. "Mostly. I was here often as a kid, but after my parents were killed, Master Hiko took me in."

"Your parents were killed at the end of the Mage Wars, right?" Swift asked, her eyes slipping shut as she finally relaxed into the water.

"Yes, the day the truce was declared." There hadn't

been time to celebrate. I hadn't found out until the following day that the war was even over. Then I hadn't wanted to believe it. My parents were honored as war heroes, of course, but everyone was so ready to put the conflict behind them that I was left grieving alone.

"I still remember hearing the news," Swift said quietly. "At the time, I was just terrified my parents would be next. Did Hiroji live with you here as well?"

"No, he only trained here a few days a week after school," I said, sinking a little lower in the hot water. "Did you have any friends growing up?"

She was silent for a moment. "Not really. Other than maybe Professor Gresham, I wouldn't say I had any friends. My parents, well...everyone wanted to know them. So, everyone wanted to know me, but they kept me pretty isolated when I was younger to prevent any appearance of favoritism or someone using me to try to influence them."

"That's pretty harsh for a kid."

She shrugged. "I'm free of all that now."

If I hadn't known, perhaps I would have missed the tension in her tone, but it was obvious to me now. "Yet, they're still trying to kill you."

I knew that wasn't true, but she had no idea yet. I'd probably have to tell her what I'd done eventually, but...not tonight.

"Sometimes family sucks," she said, her voice going hard. "Sometimes *people* just suck."

"Yeah." Swift's family certainly did. As well as Hiroji's. My parents had been good as far as I remembered. They had loved me, at least, but they were gone now and had been for over a century. "Have you found a solution to this issue with your parents?"

"Not yet," she said. "Hopefully soon. If not, I'll be out of your hair, and you can go back to working alone."

"Out of my hair how, exactly?" I asked, curious to see if she'd be honest.

She shrugged. "Does it matter?"

Master Hiko approached the *onsen*, holding his towel loosely in front of him for modesty. He stepped in at the other end, sighing in pleasure. "Feels nice after a long day of beating up my favorite student and his new partner."

I snorted. "Tomorrow we won't go so easy on you."

"See that you don't," Sakura said. "I think he is getting fat. He needs the exercise, but today he barely broke a sweat."

I blinked. She was sitting in the water less than a meter from Swift, and judging by the look on her face, she didn't have any clue how the woman got there either. That never stopped being creepy.

"I think we can make him break a sweat at least. What do you think, Lexi?" I asked with a grin.

She gave me an appraising look. "Yeah, I think we can do that much, at least. I'm pretty sure we'll land at least one, solid punch tomorrow in fact."

"Oh-ho!" Hiko leaned forward. "Care to make that a wager?" he asked, a mischievous twinkle in his eye.

Swift's mouth curled up in a smile. "Absolutely."

SIXTEEN

Swift's fist connected with Master Hiko's cheek. The thunk of bone on bone was loud. We all paused, and her eyes grew wide.

He grinned. "Good job." Then, he twisted and threw a back kick that caught Swift right in the diaphragm. She wheezed like a three-pack-a-day smoker as it lifted her off her feet and threw her into the wall.

"That is enough for now. You are still weak together, but you will learn," Master Hiko said, turning and walked out of the dojo.

Swift groaned on the floor. "I finally get a punch in, and he leaves?"

I laughed and walked over, extending a hand to help her up. "Pretty much." She wrapped her hand in mine, and I hauled her to her feet. "I learned early on that he punishes you for landing a strike. But that never stopped me from trying my hardest to do so."

She rubbed her sternum. "He's a very interesting teacher."

"That he is," I said, slapping my hand on her back. "Time for showers. You reek."

"Actually, that smell is you," Swift said, shoving me a little.

We left the dojo laughing, and I was almost irritated to find that she was starting to feel like my partner instead of a punishment.

I took a quick shower, scrubbing the sweat from my sore muscles. Part of me wanted to linger in the hot water, but we were headed to dinner after this, and hunger was definitely winning out.

Hopping out of the shower stall, I grabbed a towel and rubbed my head with it to soak up the excess water. Every time I looked in the mirror I was still a little worried my hair might be pink. Thankfully, the change back had been permanent.

I pulled the towel off my head and paused, listening closely to a familiar voice I hadn't expected to hear in this place. Pulling on pants, I hurried over to the door, moving as quietly as I could. It slid open silently, and I padded down the hall toward the sound of a quiet conversation.

They were in one of the sitting rooms. I peeked

through the cracked door and saw Yui, in her human form, standing in the center of the room with her arms crossed. Master Hiko was just out of my line of sight, but I could hear his gruff voice, speaking in Japanese. They seemed to be arguing.

"I don't believe you," Hiko said.

Yui turned her head to the right, making a displeased noise. "It doesn't matter what you believe, or what you think. It is fate. This visit was a courtesy, but I can see it was also a waste."

Swift touched my elbow, and I almost jumped out of my skin. She looked through the crack as well, then back at me. *What the hell,* she mouthed silently.

I shrugged and pulled her away from the door. Master Hiko had lied to me once already. Whatever this was, it left me with a feeling of unease. Exactly how many secrets was he keeping? And why was Yui here at all?

He had to have a reason. Maybe he would tell me soon.

SEVENTEEN

The windows of the bar were all open, but the place still stunk of cigarettes. I leaned back in my chair and tried not to breathe too deeply. A waiter dropped off the beer I'd ordered and I picked it up gratefully, glad for another distraction.

It would have been easy to slip into a bad mood with the questions rolling around in my head but, with Swift and Sakura engaged in a drinking competition, I decided to let it all be for a night. I was already six or nine — ok, so I had lost count — shots in, and the room was spinning pleasantly.

The two women were squared off on either side of a small table. Ten shots sat between them.

"Take a shot, throw a shuriken," Sakura said, dropping one by each shot. "The first one to miss the bullseye loses and is dishonored *forever*."

Swift pushed her sleeves up. "Let's do this."

"Elders first," Sakura said, grabbing a shot and throwing it back like it was water. The shot glass hit the table, then she grabbed a shuriken and whirled around. The angular black blade flew through the air, hitting the bullseye dead center. No matter how drunk she got, she never missed.

Swift didn't waste any time. She downed her shot and grabbed the shuriken, testing its weight briefly before lobbing it at the dart board. It sunk in next to Sakura's, causing it to fall to the ground.

Sakura turned her dark eyes to Swift, narrowing them in irritation. I winced. The fight was about to be on.

Yui appeared out of nowhere and sat down in the chair next to mine.

"What are you doing here?" I asked, keeping my eyes on the rivalry brewing in front of me.

"I missed you," she said, batting her eyelashes.

"What are you *actually* doing here?"

She sighed. "Just visiting. I was curious about the place you grew up. Besides, as your guardian, I should be here checking to make sure you're safe. Especially after that little run in with the Lord High Chancellor."

My fingers tightened on the beer I was holding. "Do not tell anyone about that," I warned through gritted teeth.

She patted me on the arm. "Don't worry, I'm good at secrets." She stood and sashayed toward the bar, drawing attention as she went.

The bar erupted into cheering and laughter. I turned my attention back to the competition. Empty shot glasses littered the table between Swift and Sakura. My partner was glaring at Sakura, who returned the evil look with a grin.

"You cheated! You bumped my arm," Swift said, jerking her elbow out in imitation of Sakura's interference.

Sakura shrugged, looking unrepentant. "We never said no interference."

"That's — I shouldn't have had to!"

"Accept your dishonor!" Sakura admonished, waving a shuriken in Swift's face. "You lost because I was smarter. Next time, don't assume anything about the enemy."

Swift looked back at me and gestured at the other woman. "You aren't going to back me up on this?"

Master Hiko cackled as the two women stared at me, daring me to take a side. "I, uh, wasn't watching when it happened," I said, lifting my hands in surrender. I was too drunk to navigate dangerous interactions like this one.

Swift's face was ruddy from the alcohol. She stalked

over and plopped down in the chair across from me. "You are a terrible partner."

"Hey, I've gotten better. Besides, you're worse." I finished off my beer. It should have been a water, but the more intoxicated I was, the less I had to think.

"I am not!"

"You slow me down. You're a rule follower," I said, gesturing back at Sakura who still looked like the cat who got the cream. Master Hiko was buying her shots and giving her his woo-woo eyes. I shuddered in horror and turned my attention back to Swift.

"You're just intimidated because I'm stronger than you," Swift said, narrowing her eyes.

"You're not that strong. I could take you," I said with a huff.

Swift leaned forward, looking truly insulted. "I'm the strongest."

"Wanna bet on it?" I asked, bracing my hands against the table between us.

"No bets. Just...a contest." Swift set her elbow on the table and wiggling her fingers at me. "An arm wrestling contest. I will reclaim my honor."

"We need a judge." I looked around, but didn't see anyone familiar. "You!" I said, startling a random man at the table next to ours. "We need a judge."

I turned my chair to be square with the table, and by the time I had my elbow on the table a crowd had gathered around us. Money exchanged hands in a flurry as bets were quickly made. Someone was shouting something around us, but none of that mattered. This was between me and Swift.

We wrapped our hands together. Her palm was clammy and hot. Muscles flexed in her forearm as she adjusted her grip. I shifted in my seat, bracing myself. This wasn't going to be easy.

"No magic," I said, watching her eyes carefully for a surge of pink.

Swift nodded. "No magic."

A man, drunker than either of us, slurred some instructions in Japanese that Swift couldn't understand. Then he lifted his hand, watching each of us and drawing out the moment. My heart pounded in my chest. Swift's nostrils flared as she took a deep breath. The man dropped his hand, starting the contest.

My arm tilted back as Swift ground her teeth together with a growl and pushed with all her might. I couldn't lose this. Not in front of all these people. Straining against the almost immovable force pressing against my palm, I pushed back. Inch by inch, her hand began to move.

Our entwined hands crept past the middle point, angling her fist toward the table. A grin split her face as a foot connected with my shin. I barely flinched, but it was enough. She slammed my hand back onto the table, wrenching me completely out of my chair in the process.

She jumped to her feet, threw her hands in the air, and shouted in victory. Someone handed her a foaming mug of beer. She chugged it in five quick swallows and smacked the empty glass down on the table.

"I don't always follow the rules!" she said, staring down at where I lay on the dirty floor.

"Fine," I muttered. "But I think I like you better when you're drunk."

She beamed at me and extended her hand to help me up. I let her drag me to my feet.

"If we have to part ways after all, I'll be a little sad to leave," she said, her smile fading slightly.

"Why would we have to part ways?" I asked.

Swift shook her head, forcing the smile back on her face. "Let's take more shots!"

EIGHTEEN

M y body still ached from the day before. I poked at a purple and green bruise on my wrist and winced. The hangover wasn't helping either.

Billy finally walked out of the back room clutching a set of keys. His face was still scraped, but something about him had changed. He was standing a little straighter now, like he knew his worth better. "I got it, but it was hard," he said, holding out the keys.

I took them with a grin. "You are the *man.*"

"Where's Swift?" Billy asked, leaning around me to look for her.

"On her way. She just said she was running a little behind." I tossed the keys up and caught them, resting my elbow against the counter. "How's...Jennifer? Jessica?"

"Sarah," Billy replied with a grin that said it all. "She's

great. And so smart. She's working on her runetech degree. We actually go to the same college, but since I'm in Healing, we never crossed paths. Until the unicorns. I think they're my new favorite animal."

"I can sincerely say you're the only person I've ever heard say that."

"Sorry I'm late," Swift said, jogging up to us. "Missed my train because I slept through my alarm. Glad to see you're doing okay, Billy."

"Yeah, I'm great! It's actually been really interesting healing my own injuries. I've learned a lot."

Swift laughed. "That's a good outlook on the situation."

"Billy got us a new car," I said, dangling the keys in front of her.

"You can't keep spoiling him like this," Swift said, shaking her head at us.

Billy shrugged and sat down in his desk chair. "Blackwell literally saved my life. And helped me ask out Sarah."

"See?" I said, gesturing at Billy. "I'm a hero. I deserve a nice car."

Swift rolled her eyes. "Alright, you've had your ego pumped up enough for the day. We need to go; we're already running late for the meeting with Professor Gresham. He's pulled a few books for us."

"See you next time, Billy," I said with a nod.

Swift and I hurried to the Rune Rail and slipped on the train to Seattle just in time. It was the middle of the day there so, lucky for us, we even managed to snag seats.

"Why do you think the warlock hasn't attacked again yet?" Swift asked, thinking out loud. "Could he be done?"

"I really doubt it." I shook my head. "Maybe the attacks are tied to the phases of the moon. Or he's just gathering what he needs for the next showdown. The phoenix he had to steal, but the unicorns he was able to just summon himself. Who knows what he'll use next, or where he'll strike."

"Any news from Bootstrap?"

"Not yet, but I'm hoping we'll hear from him tonight." I stretched my legs out in front of me, flexing the sore muscles. "I have this gut feeling that the next attack won't be in New York City."

"Why do you think that?" Swift asked.

I shook my head. "Not sure. Like I said, just a gut feeling. The unicorns seemed like the last strike."

"How long has it been since there was an active warlock?" Swift asked.

"That survived long enough to become public knowledge? At least thirty years," I said.

"It still baffles me that the Mage's Guild missed so

much. He should never have been able to get this powerful."

"You know, the Mage's Guild generally only hides things for one reason," I said, turning to look at her.

"Because it makes them look bad," she said, stating exactly what I was thinking.

I nodded my head. "Stopping an up-and-coming warlock makes them look good. So, assuming they knew about him, what possible reason could they have to hide his existence from the IMIB?"

Swift crossed her arms in front of her. "Because he was one of them," she said quietly.

The weight of that settled into the silence between us.

If that was true, then catching this guy would not only be difficult, but dangerous. If Bootstrap confirmed the theory, we'd have to go straight to Bradley. The fallout from Swift stealing that artifact was bad enough. This could be a disaster. The last thing either of us needed was to get any more involved with the Mage's Guild. I'd have to tell Swift what I'd done eventually, but I was going to put it off as long as possible.

My shoulder bumped into Swift's as the passenger car came to a stop. That familiar tickle of magic passed over us, and the doors slid open.

Swift shuddered. "I hate that."

"Glad I'm not the only one. It goes right through me and gives me the creeps."

We headed from the station to the garage. Swift kept checking her watch and hurrying me along, but she was the one that had made us late in the first place. She couldn't even use assassinations as an excuse now...unless those hadn't stopped for some reason.

"You weren't late today because of another assassination attempt, were you?" I asked, a little worried and pissed at the thought that those hadn't stopped even with the fine being paid.

"What?" Swift's brows pinched together. "No, I told you I slept through my alarm."

"Okay, I was just making sure that wasn't a lie for Billy's sake or something."

"No, don't worry, Blackwell. It's been a couple of days since anyone has been following me. Perhaps my parents are about to try a different strategy," Swift said with an amused smile.

It was an odd thing to joke about, but she was an odd woman.

I stopped in front of the car and narrowed my eyes. It was a...Kia Rio. What kind of trick was Billy trying to play? The car beeped as I unlocked it.

"Don't look so disappointed, Blackwell. At least it isn't yellow," Swift said with a smirk.

"Did you have something to do with this?"

Swift raised her hands in surrender. "I swear I didn't, but I can't say I'm sad about it. The near death experience must have taught Billy the value of safety."

"Do you know what Kia stands for?" I asked with a glare.

"Nothing?"

"Killed. In. Action." I yanked open the driver side door and sat down. At least the seats were leather.

Swift climbed in the other side and looked around curiously. "It's nicer than the standard issue."

"Not exactly the most exciting upgrade though," I muttered, slipping the key into the ignition. As I turned the key over, the engine roared to life.

Swift's eyes went wide. "That is *not* the standard issue engine."

"No kidding," I said, my voice full of awe. Now, American muscle wasn't exactly my thing, but I'd take that over some weak four-cylinder any day. I revved the engine again, listening to the snappy roar that echoed throughout the garage. "Good job, Billy."

"You two are ridiculous," Swift said, but the smile on her face said she liked the car just as much as I did.

"You're just jealous you don't get to drive it." I grinned and gunned it out of the spot, drowning out Swift's protest about the result of our wager. That *I* had won.

Thinking back, that could have been even worse

than having my hair turned pink. If I'd been wrong about Yui being controlled by someone, and she'd turned out to be a nogitsune, then I would have been forced to let Swift drive. Even the thought of it made me shudder in horror. I hated other people driving.

NINETEEN

Professor Gresham greeted us at the Employees Only entrance, wrapping Swift up in a tight hug. "I was worried after that unicorn attack. They're terribly nasty creatures."

"Then you'll be happy to know we killed them all," Swift said, patting him on the shoulder comfortingly.

"Blackwell, good to see you as well, though I won't embarrass you with a hug," Gresham said, smiling at me.

I snorted. "Good to see you too. And you can definitely save the hugs for Swift."

"Were you able to find much on summoning?" Swift asked.

"Yes." Gresham led us into the bookstore. "I only have one volume that discusses summoning unicorns specifically, but two others that deal with the subject as a whole. And I have a book discussing warlocks. It was written by one, in fact, which is most likely why the tome was so badly damaged."

I watched the shelves suspiciously as we walked, nervous another book might jump out at me. The last one had been annoying and cryptic. It had stopped twitching whenever I walked by though. Mostly.

"I'm surprised it survived at all," Swift said.

Gresham led us up a narrow, circular staircase to the third floor. He had stashed the books in a reading nook. Four plush chairs sat in front of a stained glass window, a table between them.

"Alright, this first one discusses the unicorns." He handed a book to Swift, then picked up another and handed it to me. The front cover had been ripped off, and the pages were extremely worn. "And this is the one written by the warlock."

Swift sat down in the farthest chair, and I took the one next to her. Laying the book out carefully on the table, I flipped through it. The author had switched between French and Spanish, even throwing in some old English. It made my brain hurt, but, like most mages, I'd had plenty of time to learn multiple languages in my long life.

My stomach twisted as I read the warlock's rantings. I could understand why someone had wanted this destroyed. It was horrible. Warlocks were power-hungry, mad with the desire to wield magic that had no place in this world. I knew what destructive, out-of-control magic felt like, and I couldn't fathom seeking it out.

I flipped to a torn page that had shown a drawing. All I could make out was an arm and half a symbol. A pile of skulls was drawn next to a figure. It was grotesque.

"Finding anything helpful?" Swift asked, leaning over to look at my book.

"Maybe, but it's mostly just reaffirming what I already knew. I hate warlocks," I said.

Swift snorted and tugged the book closer to her. "Very insightful, but not helpful to the case at all." She looked at the torn picture. "Professor, any idea who this figure might be?"

He adjusted his glasses and examined the drawing carefully. "Hmm, not off hand. I'll have to compare it to other historical drawings. My best guess is a deity of some sort. One involved in human sacrifice."

"The warlock seemed to be after something else, not specifically killing people," I said, rubbing my hand along the stubble on my jaw.

Swift stretched her arms over her head, yawning. "Yeah, if he wanted to kill people, there are better ways than summoning a phoenix. Between that and the unicorns, it's like he just wanted...chaos."

"That's definitely what he created." I drummed my

fingers against the table. "I think we should direct our focus there. On why he wanted to create chaos and if that weird amulet is somehow capturing it."

"Amulet?" Gresham asked, brightening at the promise of a new mystery.

"I'll show you," Swift said, pulling her phone out of her pocket. She flipped through her pictures until she had a clear-ish image of the thing he had used to suck my magic from me. "This drew something out of the phoenix and Blackwell."

"Really? That is very odd," Gresham said, moving the phone around until it was at the proper angle for him to see. "Surely an artifact that could drain someone of magic would have come to light much sooner. Unless it is something this warlock created?"

"We have no way of telling." Swift shrugged. "We have no idea who this warlock is, or how long he's been preparing for these attacks."

"Hopefully we can get answers to those questions soon," I said.

TWENTY

My eyes were dry and irritated from hours spent staring at small, smudged print. I wasn't sure I'd ever read that much in my life. As soon as Swift had suggested we take a break for the night, I'd practically run out of the bookstore.

Yawning, I pulled off my suit jacket and draped it over the hanger the izakaya provided. There were a few by every table for the guests so their jacket didn't have to get wrinkled or end up on the ground.

The place was packed with *salarymen* and white-haired retirees. Tables were shared by strangers, all squeezed into the small building with its low roof. It was warm inside, but all the windows were thrown open, letting in the brisk nighttime breeze.

I sat down next to an old man. His back was stooped

with age, and his face had deep wrinkles. If I had to guess his age, for a human, it'd be over one hundred.

He pushed a cup over to me. "While you wait," he said in Japanese with a polite bow of his head, which I returned.

"Thank you," I replied in the same language, a little surprised he had spoken to me in Japanese first. Most locals started with English until they learned you were fluent as a courtesy to avoid embarrassing you. Politeness reigned in Japan.

The tea was perfectly brewed. It warmed me inside and out as I drank it. Leaning back, I enjoyed the refreshment after a long week of hard work.

As a waiter walked by the table, I got his attention and ordered my usual.

"I've seen you in here before, but not very often," the old man said, refilling my tea.

"I work more than a *salaryman*," I said with a laugh. "But I stop by whenever I have time."

"Tch," he scoffed, shaking his head. "The young work until they are old, then the old are bored until they die. We live too long these days."

He had no idea. Prosaics lived well into their hundreds thanks to modern medicine and magical interventions, but supernaturals lived for centuries. I was probably older than the man sitting next to me, and some days I felt it. But other days, it felt like I was still thirty years old and trying to figure out where I was meant to fit into the world.

"A man could live forever and feel like he never made a difference," I said. Hiroji's comments were still like a splinter in my mind. The ledger containing proof of Alberto Bianchi's crimes sat in my desk drawer, taunting me daily.

"Every man has his purpose on this earth, but most don't find it. They turn away from their destiny," he said, wagging his finger at me.

"Destiny?" I raised my eyebrow, skeptical. "Do you really believe in that?"

"Do you not?"

"I —" The waiter appeared with my food. I paused to thank him and ordered a beer to go with my meal. Tea wasn't going to cut it if this old man wanted to talk about *destiny*. "Destiny, fate, it's all crap," I said, shaking my head. "A person makes the decisions they make, there is no mystical force controlling it."

"Ah, so you are a cynic." The old man leaned back, humming as though he had me all figured out.

"Not sure how you get cynic from that." I took a bite of the *kara-age*. It was perfectly fried, and the chicken was juicy and hot. This was the perfect reward for my hard work. Maybe Swift would appreciate the food in a place like this a little better than the other restaurant I'd taken her to.

"Destiny, or fate, gives people hope," the man argued. "To be born without purpose would be a depressing life. Every person should have and know their place in this world. Only a cynic would call that *crap*."

I chuckled and shook my head. "What you call fate can be cruel, too. Perhaps I'm optimistic because I don't accept that some tragedies were meant to be. I'd like to think that my choices might be able to change things for the better."

"Every young man wishes the same," he said, nodding sagely. "Let us toast to hope, whatever its source."

I opened my mouth to say I didn't have my beer yet, but the waiter set it by my hand in the same moment. Picking it up, I said, "To hope. *Kanpai!*"

We tapped bottles and I took a long drink. When I lowered the beer, the old man was gone. I looked around, confused. I hadn't thought he was a mage, but he'd disappeared just like Sakura was fond of doing.

Someone bumped the chair next to me. I turned my head and saw Hiroji leaning back slightly to allow a waiter with a tray to pass by. He saw me at the same time, and his lips thinned in irritation.

"You are haunting me today, Blackwell," he said with a sigh.

Likewise, I thought. Of all the places for him to show

up, it was hard to believe he'd walked in here on the same night as me by accident.

"I'm surprised to see you in Kichijoji. What brings you to my favorite izakaya?" I asked aloud.

Hiroji frowned, then pulled off his suit jacket and sat down next to me. "An unfortunate twist of fate."

The words set off alarm bells in my head. What were the odds? It was like drawing a full house three times in a row. It just didn't happen.

"Fate brought you here?" I asked, taking another drink of beer to steady myself.

"I was visiting a business partner in the neighborhood, but the car broke down and had to be towed. The car service can't pick me up for at least two hours. Hunger led me here." He glanced at me from the corner of his eye. "Unfortunately."

We sat silently, neither of us willing to look at the other or start a conversation. I was surprised he'd even sat down.

The waiter delivered a drink and a plate of food to Hiroji. He dug in, eating stiffly without looking like he was enjoying the meal at all.

"You knew who Swift was, and why she was being targeted," I said, finally breaking the silence. This had been bothering me since they day I'd figured it all out. "Why didn't you just tell me when you were warning me?"

"I thought you knew and were hiding it for some reason," Hiroji said, washing down a bite of food with a drink. "Why did you pay off her debt?"

I picked at the corner of the label that was peeling off the beer because of the condensation. "She did the right thing, and she was being punished for it."

"What she did was illegal," Hiroji countered.

"But it was *right*." I shook my head, frustrated. "You can't blindly follow laws."

He tapped his chopsticks on the edge of his plate in a rare display of irritation. "I never thought I'd hear you, of all people, say that."

"Just because I think what you're doing is shitty doesn't mean I don't understand that life isn't black and white."

He snorted and shook his head. "Whatever you say, *detective*."

If it was fate that brought Hiroji here tonight, then fate was an asshole determined to annoy me to death.

"Me and Swift went to Master Hiko to train a couple of days ago," I said, regretting the words as soon as they came out of my mouth.

"So, you are determined to keep her as your partner," he said, giving me an odd look.

I shrugged. "It is what it is. We needed to learn to work together. That was always easy with you when we were young."

"Back then, we understood each other."

There were several responses on the tip of my tongue. Angry ones. I swallowed them all and nodded. "Maybe one day we will again," I said, lifting my beer in a toast.

After a moment's hesitation, he lifted his as well and tapped our bottles together. "I hope so."

TWENTY-ONE

"Shouldn't you two be at work?" Yui drawled from her place on my couch, eating my cookies.

"Shouldn't you be guarding me instead of annoying me?" I tossed my things down on the table near the door.

Yui stretched out a little further and deliberately brushed some crumbs off her shirt onto the floor. I ground my teeth together and glared at her.

"You know, I think you two deserve each other," Swift said as she brushed past me.

"What's that supposed to mean?" I asked, turning my glare on her.

"You both like pissing people off."

Yui snickered around a mouthful of food.

I rolled my eyes and muttered some unflattering

things beneath my breath. "I ought to kick both of you out of my apartment."

"You'd be lost without me," Swift said, digging in my refrigerator for a drink. She was certainly making herself at home.

I shoved Yui's legs off the couch and sat down, opening my laptop. Bootstrap had contacted me about a half hour ago and told me he'd found something. We were both antsy to hear his news.

"Go find someone else to bother, Yui," I said, flicking her foot that was digging into my thigh.

She sighed. "This is basically guardian abuse."

"You'll live. I'm pretty sure all that guardian stuff is crap, anyhow."

Yui made a point of looking pathetic about it, but she got up and left the apartment. Swift brushed the crumbs off the couch and sat down next to me. After a moment, the screen flared to life.

"You didn't have to make the kitsune leave," Bootstrap whined.

"I'm not paying you to flirt with my squatter," I said.

Bootstrap huffed in annoyance. "I think you should, but, I digress. The reason I called was to tell you about the extremely interesting information I uncovered. Turns out, Mr. Scary Warlock used to be Mr. Scary Magister."

"I knew it," I said, my hands tightening on my knees.

The Mage's Guild was involved. "Did you find his name?"

"Samuel Costa."

"How long ago was he a magister?" Swift asked.

"It's been almost two years since he was employed with the Mage's Guild," Bootstrap said. A shuffling noise echoed through the speakers. "But I think he was off being naughty for a few months before he was officially dismissed. I'm sending over the information on that right now."

Swift turned to me. "We knew this was likely, but it does complicate the case."

"No joke. We have to tell Bradley right away, at least to get his opinion."

"Would you care to also hear about Costa's likely whereabouts?" Bootstrap interjected.

"You know where he is?" I asked, ready to run out the door and go find this asshole right now.

"Not at this exact moment, but I can tell you that he left New York. He *was* staying at a run-down motel in Queens. Paid cash. Cameras never saw his face, except for one at a convenience store right next door," Bootstrap said, his chair squeaking incessantly in the background.

"Any idea where he went?" Swift asked.

"I lost his trail after he took a train out of New York City. He was headed west or north, it was hard to tell. I think it's notable that he didn't go through Moira, though."

I sighed, rubbing my hand down my face. "Does he have a home base?"

"He stays pretty mobile, but he did spend a lot of time in South America in those couple of months before he went completely rogue. From what I can tell he's been in and out of Mexico more often than any other country in the past couple of years, but he was born there," Bootstrap said.

"What exactly was he doing in Mexico?" Swift asked.

"I'm glad you asked," Bootstrap said, his voice smug. "Yet again, I save the day and deliver to you: the motive of our universally disliked warlock. It's nefarious, deviously unexpected, and, dare I say it...evil."

Swift groaned at Bootstrap's grandstanding and put her face in her hands.

"Get to the point," I ground out, equally frustrated.

"Okay, okay, you two cavemen have no appreciation for a good reveal." He cleared his throat before continuing. "Based on his contacts, and the locations he went, and the money he's spent on artifacts, he worships some kind of deity...I think. Whatever he is doing, or after, is connected to this god somehow. The locals seem to treat him like some kind of priest."

Everyone, other than prosaics, knew gods and

goddesses didn't exist. Warlocks liked to use them as an excuse to commit atrocities.

Swift pulled out the books from Gresham and began flipping through them, her eyes flicking from side to side as she read. "Can you find out *exactly* what artifacts he bought? Are they magical or prosaic?"

"I found a few, which I'm sending over...now." My laptop beeped with the alert. "But some of them were shady deals in places without cameras. Not much I can do in those cases."

I looked at each picture, but none of them looked like the strange device from the other day. "You say the locals treat him like a priest. How?"

"Some of them give him offerings. Free food and board, things like that. I can't tell if it's motivated more by respect or fear, though," Bootstrap said.

"Who was his immediate superior as a magister?" Swift asked, pausing in her reading.

"Hmm." Bootstrap typed rapidly, then said, "Magister Supreme Helen Forrester."

Swift tapped her fingers against her lips, but shook her head. "I don't know her by name, but I do know someone in the office that might be able to tell me about her."

"I should probably also point out that she's dead. Killed a year ago in a tragic accident," Bootstrap said.

"An actual accident, or an assassination?" I asked. It

was likely the Mage's Guild had her killed if she had let a warlock develop under her nose or was involved with him. It was equally likely Samuel Costa had killed her to keep her quiet. Either way, this was bad news. A magister was hard to kill. A magister supreme was even harder.

"Always so hard to say when the Guild is involved. If it was an assassination, it was a clean one."

Swift turned to me. "As much as we want to get to the bottom of what the Mage's Guild is hiding, we need to focus on the warlock himself."

I sighed, but nodded in agreement. "I know. Boot-strap, if the warlock pops up again, contact me *imme-diately.*"

"You got it, payer-of-my-school-loans," Bootstrap replied, a grin in his voice.

TWENTY-TWO

I'd sent Bradley the coded message over an hour ago. He knew it meant to meet me at our designated spot, to come alone, and to make sure no one followed. It was something he had insisted on with all his agents. We each had our own, special code word. If there was ever a question of what we could say at the office, we had been instructed to use it and tell him in private.

The bar, located in the maze of New York City, catered to supernaturals. It was an old haunt, one used back when we hid from prosaics. It had been built with secrets in mind. The chatter in the bar was muted. Every booth was a complete dead zone; no signal or sound got in or out. There were backrooms where shady deals were conducted, and no one asked questions. They also had good ale.

"Two pints of the strongest ale you have," I said, sliding two bills across the squeaky clean bar.

The bartender snatched up my cash wordlessly and pulled the drafts. She handed me the foaming pints with a polite nod. Swift had already gotten her drink and claimed a booth for our meeting.

I slid in beside her, setting one of the ales on the opposite side of the table for Bradley.

"He should be here by now," Swift said, her fingers gripping her glass tightly.

"It's fine," I said, nudging her with my elbow. "He has to make it look casual. If he ran out of the office, he'd arouse suspicion. Besides, he might be in a meeting."

A waitress walked over and set a basket of unidentifiable fried food on the end of our table. Swift reached past me and dragged it toward her. "Finally, I'm starving."

She popped a morsel in her mouth and hummed in satisfaction.

"What is it?" I asked, poking at the contents of the basket.

She glared at me and tugged it away. "Fried pickles."

I frowned and sat back. She could have them. That sounded awful. "You don't appreciate a fine meal cooked to perfection, but you look like you're in heaven from eating *fried pickles?*"

Swift stuffed two more in her mouth and shrugged. "I like what I like."

The door to the bar opened, and a wide man blocked out the sunlight for a moment. Bradley let the door swing shut behind him as he searched the space for me. I waved my hand and he lumbered toward us.

He gave Swift only a cursory glance as he slid into the booth, apparently unsurprised to see her here. "My two favorite troublemakers," Bradley said with narrowed eyes that implied otherwise.

I slid the ale toward him. "Have a drink, old man."

He snorted, but took a long drink nonetheless, perhaps steeling himself for the coming conversation. "What do you need to tell me that you can't tell me in Moira?" Bradley asked, setting down the pint. His mustache had caught some of the foam, which was slowly dripping off one side.

"Samuel Costa. That's the name of our warlock. A little over a year ago, he went by *Magister* Samuel Costa." As I said it, Bradley's lips pressed together, causing his mustache to fluff out.

"A magister turned warlock. What a shit storm. Were the unicorns not enough? You had to bring me this bad news too?" Bradley demanded, throwing his hands in the air.

"His supervisor died in an accident about a year ago," Swift said, letting the implication hang between us.

Bradley would be able to see the possibility that it was an assassination, and that it may not have been the Mage's Guild that killed her.

"Now the Guild is holding back information on this warlock." Bradley sighed, shaking his head. "You know it's not yet time for all this to come to light, Lexi."

My brows pinched together. *Lexi?* He said it like they were old friends.

"I know," she said, her shoulders slumping. "You needed to know, regardless. They're going to be watching our every move on this case."

"They're already watching your every move," Bradley said with a shrug.

"It's not time for what to come to light?" I asked, feeling the old agitation at being left out of the loop.

Bradley exchanged a glance with Swift, who nodded her head as if she were giving him permission.

"You know as well as anyone that corruption in the Mage's Guild runs deep. Swift came to me over a year ago. I've known her since she had acne and a bad perm, and I knew she was telling the truth about the things she had seen working in Magical Artifacts. One day, in the distant future, we may be able to expose and root out the corruption. But it's not this day and not this case." Bradley picked up his ale and chugged the rest. He set down the empty mug with a burp.

"When were you planning on telling me about this?"

I ground out. After everything I had done for Swift, this was how she repaid me? To be fair, she didn't know about that, but *still*. It rankled.

Bradley just shrugged. "I figured the opportunity would present itself. And I was right."

"So you really did arrange for me to be Swift's bodyguard once she was fired," I said, keeping my eyes fixed on the Chief. I didn't particularly want to look at my partner right now.

"You needed a partner, she needed backup. Now, you sort of work well together," Bradley stood, keeping just inside the silenced area. "Keep your eyes and ears open. Don't give them any sign we know what they did. Now is not the time to tip our hand."

Swift and I remained quiet as he nodded and left the bar. Mindlessly, I grabbed a fried pickle and ate it. She was right, it was pretty good.

"It was too big to risk at first," Swift said.

I held up my hand. "No need to explain. You did the right thing, and now I know."

"I need you to understand." Swift's tone was hard. Demanding almost.

Turning my head, I looked her in the eye. "Fine, go ahead."

"When I was a young adult, barely in my twenties, I discovered the true character of my parents. It's always a shock to realize your parents aren't perfect. It's even more of a shock to find out they are bad." She paused, twirling the half-empty glass in her hands. "Everything I've done since then has been to get out from under their control and to find a way to remove them from their positions. They have to be stopped."

I picked at a groove in the table, thinking about what she had said. "You're doing all this, even though they're your family?"

"Have you ever heard the saying 'blood is thicker than water'?" she asked.

I nodded. "Sure, it's a common saying."

"It's misleading. The full saying goes like this 'the blood of the covenant is thicker than the water of the womb,'" she said, leaning back against the booth. "I may be related to my parents, but the bonds forged with the people you fight alongside will always be strongest. That's who I choose, not them."

She was giving up a lot. More than most people even suspected, and all for a sense of justice. Of *rightness*.

"I'm glad you have a decent moral compass, or you'd be a really scary warlock," I said.

Swift smiled, understanding the acceptance. She held out her hand. "For once, let's shake as partners, instead of for a wager."

I smirked and wrapped my hand around hers. Her strength and determination were evident in her grip. I respected it and understood it.

Someone associated with the Mage's Guild had killed my parents. I was almost sure of it. Nothing else explained Master Hiko's constant attempts to discourage my investigation into their death. We were both after the same thing, and one day, I was pretty sure we'd be successful.

TWENTY-THREE

We were on level fifteen of Moira and halfway back to the IMIB when my phone rang. The caller ID was blank.

"Blackwell," I said in lieu of a greeting.

"Dude, start running. You have six minutes to get to the Boston Rune Rail or you won't make it in time for the next train," Bootstrap said, a surprising urgency in his voice.

I took off at a run. Swift sprinted after me without even questioning it.

"Where is he?"

"I'm sending you the exact coordinates. I think he's been here before, sometime when I wasn't watching him. And I don't have a good feeling about what he's doing." Bootstrap was tapping against something nervously in the background.

"Call me again if he leaves."

"Got it." Bootstrap disconnected the call.

"Has the attack already started?" Swift asked, starting to outpace me.

"No, but it's probably going to start soon."

We finally had a chance to stop this guy before he got started. My heart was pounding as much from anticipation as it was the running. The distance was farther than I liked to run, but I pushed myself. Swift and I didn't speak. We were both focused on reaching our destination; there'd be time to talk on the Rune Rail.

We jumped over the turnstile, flashing our badges to the security guards. They waved us along, used to the antics of IMIB agents.

I was glad Bootstrap had called when he had. The Rune Rail pulled into the station as we jogged down the stairs. We weren't lucky enough to find seats this time. Instead, we stood near the door trying to catch our breath.

"We need backup. There's no telling what he might be summoning this time," Swift said between pants. She wiped the back of her hand across her mouth, brushing away the sweat beading on her upper lip. Her face was flushed, and mine probably was too.

I pulled out my phone, texting Lopez and Danner. Next, I let Bradley know we had a chance to stop this guy. "I wish we knew what the damn device was. We need to get it away from him. Or destroy it."

"We can't risk destroying it without knowing what it is. There's no telling what that could unleash," Swift said, shaking her head.

"Might be better to risk that versus letting him use it," I said, leaning back against the door.

She groaned in annoyance. "I need to figure out what it is so we know what's safe. I hate not knowing."

"You and me both."

"Where are we going, by the way? Besides Boston?" she asked

"I'm not sure, Boot..." I cleared my throat. "I was given GPS coordinates, not an address. That must mean it's not in a building," I said, showing her the message and mentally kicking myself for nearly blurting out his name on the Rune Rail.

She pulled up the map on her tablet and typed in the coordinates, then looked up slightly confused. "That's in the middle of the Ted Williams Tunnels that lead from the airport to East Boston."

I leaned over to look as well. "How are we supposed to get there?"

My phone dinged with a second message.

```
Service      entrance     42.350007,
-71.031696
```

"Can he hear us?" Swift asked with narrowed eyes.

"I have no idea," I said, shaking my head. I wouldn't put it past him, but I really hoped he couldn't. The train slowed, and the wave of magic passed through us, making me shudder.

"I have the directions, just follow me," Swift said.

I nodded and got ready to run again.

TWENTY-FOUR

The tunnels were dark, lit only by thin strips of yellow lights on the ceiling. A steady stream of cars whipped past us on the busy road that lay under Boston. I opened the door to the service tunnel. It swung outward, and the smell of mold washed over me. We crept inside, my eyes slowly adjusting to the darkness around us.

Bootstrap's map had seemed simple, but here, in this musty tunnel, I wondered if we'd ever find the warlock. Our footsteps echoed off the concrete no matter how quietly we walked.

Swift tugged on my elbow, motioning for me to pause. She drew an intricate rune, the orange magic sparking from her fingertip. Magic wrapped around us like gauze, muffling the outside world. "A silencing rune. It'll move with us."

"Good call," I said, my voice still in a whisper. Despite knowing the spell would hold, it felt wrong to talk loudly.

We followed the service tunnel to the fork, then a short flight of stairs. I slowed as the sound of chanting drifted toward us. Each word was as heavy as a drum beat. The warlock's voice thrummed with dark, ancient magic. I could feel the age of it down to my bones.

"How long until Danner and Lopez get here?" Swift whispered.

"Too long. We can't let him finish what he's doing. There's no telling what he might summon this time."

She nodded in agreement. "Alright. Then I need you to create a distraction so I can attack. You have to stay hidden, or you could be vulnerable to that amulet."

I wanted to refuse. Letting her take all the risk galled me, but it was the best plan we had. "Fine, but you won't be able to overpower him by yourself. I'll have to risk it at some point."

"Just wait as long as you can."

I nodded, and Swift crept forward. The warlock stood in a small open area where three service tunnels connected. We were approaching him from behind. Past him, glimpses of the altar were visible. Skulls. Fire. The head of a bird. He was certainly taking this false god stuff seriously. Incense and the copper-penny smell of blood made my stomach roll.

The warlock was hidden behind dark robes, but his magical signature was not. It was oppressively powerful, and I could feel the corruption in it. Oddly, it felt like not all of the magic was his. Maybe he had stolen it from other mages with that device.

A black, undulating mist rose from the surface of the altar. The warlock's chants grew louder, and magic crackled in the air.

"We can't wait," Swift whispered urgently.

"I can create a distraction, but you're not going to like it," I said as I quickly traced a few runes into the ground in front of me. We needed something to prevent him from running off once we started the fight.

"Try to drive him in this direction once we attack."

"Do not blow up these tunnels. We're literally under the ocean." Swift's eyes flashed as she narrowed them at me.

"I'll do my best," I said, moving in front of her. I lowered my hands to just a few inches off the ground and created a small, flaming sphere. It was packed full of energy and ready to blow but wasn't big enough to actually cause any damage. I hoped. "Go as soon as you see the flames."

Swift nodded, mace already in hand.

I flicked the sphere, and it rolled past the warlock and the altar. The warlock's head was tipped backward as he gestured toward the ceiling, so it managed to slip by unnoticed. I counted to five, then curled my hand into a fist. The pop of the explosion came first, followed by fire that rolled out of the tunnel opposite us.

In a fraction of a second, three not-so-great things happened. The warlock turned, looking directly at us despite the distraction. The entire tunnel began shaking as magic poured out of the altar. And Swift charged in, leaping through the air.

"I'm going to strangle you with your own dress!" she shouted, her mace blazing brightly overhead. She really needed to work on her insults.

The warlock swiped his hand toward her, sending a blast of dark magic, but she was ready for the attack this time. She smashed straight through it and landed in front of him. Without a pause, she swung upward, coming less than an inch from catching the evil bastard in the jaw.

Before he could retaliate, the altar exploded outward. I was tossed a few meters down the tunnel from the force of the shockwave. Scrambling to my feet, I ran back toward my partner. She was nowhere in sight, but the warlock was peeling himself off the wall.

The air above the altar twisted into a vortex that pulsed with dark energies. It almost looked like the portal the Rune Rail went in and out of, though it was dark instead of bright.

The warlock rose to his full height and ran forward,

then lifted the amulet hanging on a chain around his neck. I didn't wait for him to use it; I just ran toward the tunnel opposite me. Halfway there, a pink blur dropped from the ceiling.

Skidding to a halt, I quickly activated the rune I had drawn before the fight started. A wall of fire erupted from the ground, creating an impassable barrier. Swift was driving the warlock backward, but there was nowhere for him to go. He stopped, trapped between the wall of fire that was quickly growing larger and Swift's mace.

A hissing noise permeated the room. I turned toward the altar slowly. The large, green head of some creature that looked half dragon and half snake slithered out of the vortex. Followed by another. And another. And another.

"Swift, it's a hydra!" I shouted.

A head snapped at her, but she smacked it away with the staff of her mace. I charged in, drawing my katana and thrusting it at the closest head in one fluid motion. The creature shrieked in pain as the sword pierced its scaly hide.

Instead of retreating, the thing pulled itself farther out of the portal, blocking my view of Swift and the warlock. Clawed feet dug into the concrete, and the heads writhed, foot-long fangs dripping with venom.

I attacked with abandon, lopping off the first head

with a single strike. A new head began growing in its place immediately, but it looked like it might take a minute or two to fully reform. I sliced through two more, working my way onto its back. Swift couldn't fight that warlock on her own. I had to get to her.

"He's running!" Swift shouted.

The warlock darted past the hydra and ran down a different tunnel. I drove my sword down into the back of the hydra. It screeched, and the heads twisted around trying to bite me.

Swift jumped on its back and hit one, then shoved me toward the tunnel. "We have to go after him!"

"What about the hydra?" I shouted back, following her. One of the heads hit the concrete wall as it flailed.

"It'll follow!"

As we ran down the tunnel, concrete cracked loudly behind us. The hydra's body was too large to fit through the opening, but that wasn't stopping it.

The door leading out of the tunnel banged open, and the warlock ran straight out into the oncoming traffic. Car horns blared as people swerved around the unexpected obstacle. A car smashed into the tunnel wall, knocking the vehicle in front of it into a tailspin. He casually gestured down the wide street and flipped over a truck that was skidding toward him.

"You have failed once again!" the warlock shouted at us.

Traffic had stopped completely. People were getting out of their cars and running in the opposite direction. That was one way to evacuate the tunnels.

"You're not getting away this time," I shouted back.

The hydra screeched behind us and slammed itself against the doorway that prevented it from reaching its prey. That wouldn't hold for long. We couldn't kill the hydra and stop the warlock from escaping.

The warlock stretched both arms wide, and green fire poured from his palms. It crept over the wreckage around him, then began to consume the line of cars that were trapped in the tunnel with us. "Blessed be the sacrifices."

The amulet flared to life on his chest as it absorbed power from the chaos around him. "My task is not finished, but we will meet again," he said with a dark smile.

The wall behind us gave way and showered us with rubble. I whipped around and barely deflected a strike from the hydra. Two heads snapped at me. I hacked off one head and stabbed the other, but I had to jump back to avoid a spray of acidic saliva.

"He's gone!" Swift shouted.

I lopped off the other head, then looked around. In that moment of distraction, the warlock had run. He'd gotten what he needed and left us with a hydra to kill.

TWENTY-FIVE

For every head we chopped off, two more sprung up in its place.

"Stop cutting off the heads!" Swift shouted as she crushed one beneath her hammer. The neck still writhed, slinging the bloody mess around with a wail.

"Yeah, I figured that out, thanks," I shouted back, irritated. We weren't tripping over each other this time, but we weren't making any progress killing this overgrown snake, either. "You know all this mythology stuff. How do we kill it?"

"That's hotly contested," she said with a grunt as she bashed in two more heads. The other one was already regrowing, a new head pushing out of the smashed bits.

"Just pick the theory you like best and let's test it!" I weaved under the mess of heads and tried striking at the body directly. My blade pierced its skin easily, but the wound closed almost immediately.

"What the hell are you two idiots doing?"

I looked back and saw a *very* welcome sight. Lopez and Danner were here. It had taken them long enough.

"We're fighting an immortal creature of darkness, what are you doing just standing there?" I called back with a grin.

Lopez rolled her eyes and began to shift into a large black panther while flame wrapped around Danner's fists.

He cracked his knuckles and jumped down off the car he was standing on. "You got a plan?"

"Ask Swift," I said, darting back in to stab the hydra's body a few more times. Maybe we could wear it out.

"To stop the heads from regenerating," Swift paused and batted away the hydra's strikes. "I think we need to cauterize the neck."

"That's it?" I asked in surprise.

"The other theory is that you have to use the hydra's venom to stop the regrowth, but this way is easier," Swift said, dodging underneath a swing of the hydra's tail. "If it works at all."

"Whatever, let's try it," I said, adjusting my grip on the katana. "I'll slice if you and Danner can burn! Lopez, can you distract the extra heads?"

She roared her approval and ran in, attacking with

claws and teeth. Three heads hissed and began focusing on her. She led them on a chase, darting back and forth under cars. Every time one got close, she raked a massive claw across its slitted nostrils.

I slipped under the head closest to me and cut it off near the base. Swift's mace, blazing with pink flames, hit the freshly made wound, searing it. I cut off the next, and the next, while my partner followed behind me.

"Is it working?" I asked, barely pausing in my attack. There were so damn many of them now.

"Yes!" Swift crowed victoriously. "Chop faster!"

I was amazed that it was actually working. It was so simple. Well...as simple as fighting over twenty venomous heads attached to a giant monster could be.

After that, it was lop and sear. Over and over until I thought my arms were going to fall off. Every time Swift had to beat a head back to give me room to work, Danner was there with his own flames, searing off the stump. We moved like one person, never in each other's way, never stopping.

As the last head fell, a shudder ran through the hydra. It swayed left, then right, before stumbling and falling. One of the severed heads still writhed on the ground.

"Why can't dead things just stay still," I muttered, glaring at it.

Swift snorted, then walked over and brought her mace down on it. It stopped wiggling.

"Did you two go to couples therapy or something?" Lopez asked, strolling toward us as a human once again. I'd never understood how it worked, but changing into their animal form didn't destroy a shifter's clothes. Magic was weird like that. "You actually managed to fight the monster instead of each other."

"Ha ha," I said drily.

TWENTY-SIX

The cleanup crew arrived to get rid of the body of the hydra. Apparently it had to be burned to ash, or there was a slight chance it might come back to life.

We, however, were headed back to the altar the thing had been summoned from. There were lots of questions that needed answers, and there was a chance the warlock had left something behind that might explain why he was doing all this. Even for a warlock, it was odd.

Swift's red trench coat was all I could see ahead of me in the dim lighting of the tunnel. The hydra's rampage had broken most of the lighting.

Once we reached the area the hydra had been summoned in, Swift drew a simple rune that produced a bright orb. She pushed it upward, lighting the room. The altar still stood in all its gruesome, bloody glory.

There were symbols, some that looked like hiero-glyphics and some I just didn't recognize, carved into the base of the altar.

"It smells like old blood and magic in here," Lopez said, her nose wrinkling in disgust.

Danner searched the perimeter, casting runes here and there to note what he found for the agents that would come and collect the evidence.

I walked up to the altar, stepping over the skulls that encircled it. The top of it was a rectangular slab of stone. It was covered in bones and runes that had been carved into the stone itself. The bones were arranged in a specific pattern rather than tossed on top. In the center lay three shriveled lumps.

"Are these...human hearts?" I asked, leaning over to get a closer look.

Swift hurried to my side and looked at them. "I think they are." She turned to Lopez. "Would you be able to tell?"

Lopez grimaced but nodded. "I'll be able to tell if they're human, at least. And if they're mage, shifter, or something else." She walked over, taking care not to disturb anything around the altar.

Swift and I stepped back, giving her room. I did not envy her this task. Sniffing random, crusty body parts wasn't anyone's idea of a good time.

Since she was so short, she barely had to lean over.

Closing her eyes, she inhaled deeply, smelling each one in turn. Her frown deepened. Stepping away from the altar, she rubbed her nose like it itched. "Those are from mages. Most likely their hearts, but it could be a different internal organ, I guess."

"That must have been what took him so long to prepare for this attack." I dragged my hand down my face. He had disappeared after the last attack and killed three mages right under our noses.

"This is a very specific sort of sacrifice. We should be able to dissect this altar, the runes, and the ritual and gain more insight into the deity he thinks he is offering it to," Swift said, pulling out her tablet to take notes.

"I actually recognize some of this," Lopez said, pointing at the circle of skulls. "The Aztecs often laid out the skulls of their enemies, and they would be placed on a rack, called a *tzompantli,* with other sacrifices." She pointed at the hearts next. "They also removed the hearts while their enemy was still alive and offered them as a burnt sacrifice to whatever god they were trying to appease."

"Interesting," Swift said, quickly writing down everything Lopez said. "My first guess was going to be Hindu, perhaps a Kali worshipper."

"Sometimes these assholes draw inspiration from several cultures," Danner said, still walking the perimeter. "They aren't picky when it comes to justifying their murders."

"That's true," Swift said, pursing her lips. She turned to Lopez. "Is there anything else that looks specifically Aztec to you?"

My phone buzzed with a text. I pulled it out, surprised to see a message from Viktor.

```
Urgent.  Come  to  morgue.  Tell
no one.
```

"Swift," I said, interrupting their conversation. "I just remembered we need to get to that meeting while we still can. Sorry, Lopez."

"Oh, right," Swift said without missing a beat. That training really had paid off. "Take all the pictures you can, we'll have to talk about it tomorrow."

Lopez nodded and waved us away.

Swift followed me back out to the car, tensely silent until she had her door shut. "What is so urgent that we needed to run out of there like that?"

I showed her the message.

"That can't be good," she said, buckling her seatbelt.

"That's an understatement. He's never texted me before, no matter how important the case."

TWENTY-SEVEN

We walked into the coroner's office, but Viktor wasn't there yet. The room was empty, no bodies in sight. I frowned, wondering where he was. He'd made it sound important and time sensitive.

Swift made a gagging noise in the back of her throat.

"There isn't even a dead body this time," I said, looking at her incredulously.

She pressed her hand to her mouth and swallowed, shaking her head. "That smell is so bad. Why does he even have Pop-Tarts in the morgue? He shouldn't be eating around all those chemicals and germs and *dead bodies.*"

"Because he's Viktor," I said, laughing at her.

"It is an easy snack," the Russian necromancer said as he walked up behind us.

Swift jumped and turned to face him with a slight

blush on her cheeks. "That...uh...makes perfect sense," she said politely.

Viktor looked at her coldly before turning to me. He *really* didn't like her. He lifted his finger, quieting us, then traced a complicated series of runes in the air. The lights dimmed slightly, and the sounds from outside the door went silent.

I watched him, slightly nervous. "Is something wrong?"

"I found an odd thing," he said, pulling open an unmarked door. He drew out a body draped in a white sheet. "As is policy, I told my supervisor. Less than an hour later I was *instructed* to pass off the case to the Mage's Guild and purge my records." He pulled back the sheet. The corpse was a man, middle-aged, with dark brown hair. Viktor tilted the man's head to the side, revealing a mark branded into the back of his neck. It looked...familiar.

Swift's hesitancy vanished, and she crouched down by the body, peering at the scar. "That's the same design that's on the device we've been seeing." She pulled out her phone and took a picture. "Any other marks?"

"No marks, but the victim's heart was pulled out through his chest." Viktor drew the tray out farther and pulled down the sheet to reveal the gruesome wound. "The wound indicates he was alive when this operation was performed."

Swift immediately stepped back and turned away. That confirmed this was the work of the warlock, though. They'd found three hearts on the altar. Each one had been burned, shriveled, and unidentifiable.

"I guess that solves the issue of at least one of our dead mages." I took her phone and snapped a few pictures. "They tried to hide this? Have there been any more?"

"There may have been. Another coroner mentioned an odd body passing through, but he didn't care to explain what was odd about it." Viktor glanced at his watch. "A magister is coming to collect the body soon. We only have a few minutes left before you must leave."

"Did you get an ID on the body?" Swift asked, still facing the door.

"He's a low ranking Guild employee named David Johnson. His license was in his pocket," Viktor said with a shrug.

"Did you get a chance to interrogate him?" I asked.

"I tried, but he would not wake." Viktor re-covered the corpse and pushed it back into the storage drawer. "You must go now. Neither of you should risk being discovered."

"Thank you, Viktor." I nodded at the burly man. We weren't exactly friends, but I liked him. He had a very black and white sense of right and wrong. I was glad he had called despite the chance of getting caught.

"Don't thank me, just stop this warlock, Blackwell," Viktor said, waving us toward the exit. As Swift opened the door, the spell Viktor had cast ended, and the sounds came rushing back to us.

We walked quickly down the hall. Everything about this case tied it to the Mage's Guild. I hated that our hands were tied. We couldn't even talk about what we'd just discovered without leaving the IMIB.

As we stepped out into the artificial sunlight of Moira, my phone rang. My estate manager's number showed on the caller ID. "Personal call, give me a moment," I said.

Swift nodded and I turned away, answering the call.

"Mr. Zamora, I hope this is good news," I said. He'd been handling liquidating my assets to cover the fine, and he wouldn't call unless it was important.

"Indeed it is, Mr. Blackwell," he replied. "Though I consider it very unwise to sell your family's home, I can at least rest easy knowing that it was sold for almost twice the asking price."

"Who the hell would buy it for more than the asking price?" I wanted to accept the good news, but my gut was telling me something was wrong.

"A surprising client, I can assure you. It was the Lord High Chancellor Swift. I even had the honor of meeting him when the paperwork was signed..."

Zamora kept prattling on, but I didn't listen to a

word he said. My fingers gripped the phone so hard it almost cracked. I hated having to sell the home in the first place. Knowing that Swift's father would have it made me want to punch something.

"Alright, great. I'll check in later if I need to know more," I said, cutting him off. He sputtered in indignation, but I just hung up the phone. His idea of 'an honor' and mine were really different.

"Everything okay?" Swift asked, walking up behind me.

She hadn't asked me to do any of this. I took a deep breath and tried to put it out of my mind. It didn't matter. The Mage's Guild covering up their connection to a warlock at the expense of our case? That mattered. It affected innocent people.

"Yeah, it's fine," I said, shoving my phone back in my pocket. "What time is it in Seattle? I think we might need to visit your friend, Professor Gresham, again."

"I think it's midnight there. We should get some rest. Should we meet at your apartment tomorrow morning to discuss...things?" Swift asked, concern still apparent on her face.

"Yeah, let's do that," I said, dragging my hand down my face. I couldn't deny that I was tired.

TWENTY-EIGHT

When I'd gotten home the night before, I'd been relieved that Yui wasn't there. For once, the apartment was quiet like it should be. I'd fallen asleep as soon as my head hit the pillow and slept like a baby.

But...she still wasn't back this morning. Stuffing another Oreo in my mouth, I stared at the empty couch. I wasn't exactly worried, but it wasn't like her to be gone this long. I should just appreciate the fleeting moments of peace while I had them.

There was a quick knock at the door before it opened. Swift walked in, shrugging off her trench coat as she nodded in greeting. "Oreos for breakfast?"

I swallowed and grabbed another cookie. "Everyone has their vices."

She snorted. "So, dead mages. Hearts cut out while they're still alive. That's not exactly normal."

"When dealing with a warlock, there is no normal," I said, tossing the empty cookie package in the trash. "I was thinking about that this morning, though. There are all sorts of summoning spells, but most don't require human sacrifice. Why did the warlock need the hearts of mages?"

"Human sacrifice was common a few centuries ago, before the Mage Wars. Back when everyone believed in the pantheon of deities." Swift began pacing the length of the living room.

"But they don't actually exist." I said. I hadn't believed in gods since I was a child. Many mythical creatures existed and appeared every now and then. But gods had never been seen by anyone. Even the oldest of beings had not met a god.

She was silent for a moment before saying, "I'm not sure that's entirely accurate."

"Oh, come on. You can't be serious!"

"These warlocks tap into something more powerful than any mage. It's always connected to something like this. Whether you want to call it a god or not, there is some kind of...sentient...*thing* out there," Swift said, gesturing sharply when she couldn't find the right words.

"I just don't buy it. We don't understand magic, but that doesn't mean there are deities out there controlling it," I said, shaking my head.

A sudden, suffocating pressure surrounded me. I choked, barely able to breathe. Swift stumbled, and magic flared at her fingertips. It must have been affecting her, too.

My first thought was that another assassin had come, but then the world around us changed abruptly. My senses were overwhelmed by the smells of the *izakaya* I had visited the night before. Swift sat across from me, her eyes wide.

"Where are we?" she asked quietly, apparently only able to move her mouth.

"Did you already forget our first meeting?"

Sitting next to me was the old man I'd met in the *izakaya*. He turned his wrinkled face to me. This time, it was obvious he wasn't human, though he still seemed old.

"How are you doing this? What are you?" I demanded, my hands clenched into fists. It was the only movement I was capable of.

"I am a god," he said, his voice seeping into me as though he wanted to force me to believe what he was saying.

Everything shifted again. A breeze sent Swift's hair dancing around her face. We stood in Master Hiko's dojo, facing the self-proclaimed god once again. I knew this place like the back of my hand. Every detail, down to the persistent smell of sweat and the knick in the wall, was accurate. It was as if this thing had plucked it straight from my mind.

The old man's features twisted as it changed forms, now masquerading as my teacher. "You are full of questions and equally full of doubt, Logan Blackwell. When we dined together at your *izakaya*, I tried to open your mind to the truth."

"You talked a lot about fate, but none of this makes it real," I said angrily, still unable to really move.

Swift was breathing hard, like she was fighting against something. I suspected this *thing* wasn't allowing her to speak.

"I am Fate, the Moirai that creates destiny," it said, anger leaking into its voice. "I am Kismet, Maat, The Norns. Your belief or disbelief means nothing." In a flash of light, it changed forms again, shifting to a woman. Sakura. "Perhaps she was right, and you are too full of chaos to be taught."

"What do you want?" I asked through gritted teeth.

It spread its hands and smiled. "I want to guide you to your destiny. Did you think it was chance that brought the two of you together? Or chance that you were born with the burden of the mayhem magic?"

"Yes, actually."

Fake-Sakura shook her head, looking disappointed in my response. "I have been involved in your life from the beginning, nudging what I could, laying out opportunities for you. Everything has led to this moment. This is the beginning of our work together. A test of sorts."

"A test for what?" I wanted to shut this creature up, but I had to know what it wanted at least.

The impostor walked toward Swift, circling her while we were still unable to move. Swift's fingers twitched, little sparks of magic forming at her fingertips. It was a futile effort.

There was something wrong about this place. I couldn't even feel my magic; it was like we weren't really here.

"A test to see if you are ready. There is a war coming, and we are all gathering our weapons."

That didn't sound good. It also didn't sound like the kind of thing I wanted to be a part of.

"A war between who? Mages?"

Fate shook its head. "No, between the immortals."

Then, the thing — Fate, I guess — just vanished, and we were back in my apartment. The oppressive force dissipated, and I stumbled forward, looking for Swift just to make sure she'd made it back from wherever that was as well.

TWENTY-NINE

"**D**id that just happen?" Swift asked, her face still flushed from exertion.

I looked around my apartment, but whatever it was seemed to be gone. "Yeah, it did. My hand still aches from trying to punch that thing," I said, flexing my fingers.

"This changes everything," she said angrily, beginning to pace back and forth. "If gods exist, whether they match up with our concept of what gods are or not, it just..." she shook her head. "We couldn't touch Fate. We couldn't escape its illusion. It froze me without even blinking. None of what just happened should be possible."

Anger rushed through me. I turned and smacked the nearest thing off the kitchen counter. The toaster hit the wall with a crash and broke, the pieces clattering to the floor. I was in control of my life, not some self-appointed deity. And definitely not *fate*.

"I'm going to strengthen my wards and do everything possible to keep that thing away from me." Taking a deep breath, I turned back to Swift. There was nothing we could do about the god right now, but we had learned something important. "This warlock is tapping into something real. We aren't going to be able to take it down alone. I think we need to ask for help."

Swift took a moment to collect herself, then nodded. "From whom?"

"Master Hiko and Sakura."

She pinched her brows together. "Will they help?"

I shrugged. "I think so. No matter their answer, we have to ask. There is another person we need to talk to as well."

"Who?" Swift asked, squaring her shoulders.

"Yui. She was conspicuously absent today, almost like she was avoiding something. And when she showed up at Master Hiko's, I heard her mention fate. It didn't seem important until now."

"It's possible Fate banished her somehow. Some guardian she is," Swift muttered, sitting down heavily on the couch. "Regardless of how I feel about Fate, we need to find out everything we can about these other immortals or gods. I think we should go to Mexico City. Costa has spent a lot of time there. It's possible there are clues to his goals, and that device, in the city."

I nodded in agreement. "I think we should ask Lopez to come with us. She recognized some of the imagery, and we could use an outside perspective on this."

"I know he isn't an IMIB agent, but I'd like to ask Professor Gresham to come with us as well. He has hundreds of years of experience studying mythology, and before he opened the bookstore, he was actually an archaeologist," Swift said, leaning forward to rest her elbows on her knees.

"He has been helpful. It might be dangerous, though. Are you sure it's safe for him to come?" I asked, my brows pinched in concern.

Swift laughed. "Yeah, he'll be just fine."

I crossed my arms. "We can't tell anyone about what happened today. Not even Lopez and Gresham."

"Because they'll think we're crazy?" she asked, raising her eyebrow.

"Not just that. I don't think it's safe for them to know."

Swift sighed, rubbing her hand across her face. "Fate said a war is coming. We may need all the allies we can get."

"We'll tell them when the moment is right, but there is too much we don't know. We aren't sure we can even trust anything Fate said."

For the first time since moving here, my apartment didn't feel safe. My own mind didn't feel safe. Fate had known things it shouldn't have. It had been able to control both of us without any sign of effort.

I looked down at my hand, flexing my sore fingers. That must have been how Yui felt the entire time Murray had her ball. If she had fled from Fate, I couldn't blame her.

THIRTY

Lopez met us on level seven of Moira, by the Rune Rail platform that would take us to Mexico City. She had a backpack slung over her shoulder, prepared for a one night stay, and wore jeans instead of her usual suit. We were planning on posing as tourists instead of IMIB agents.

"If my mother finds out I've come home without seeing her, she's going to murder me," Lopez said, nodding in greeting. "So no one better find out about this."

Swift laughed. "We'll do our best to stay inconspicuous."

Lopez narrowed her eyes. "Coming from you two, that doesn't exactly fill me with confidence." A loud clanging echoed through the platform, drawing closer and closer to us. "What the hell is..."

We were all struck silent as Professor Gresham approached. He wore a wide-brimmed sable fedora with a large red feather stuck to the side and a khaki jumpsuit tucked into hiking boots. A monstrous backpack stuck up above his head, stuffed to the brim with who knew what. Two cast iron pots hung off the side, banging together with every step he took. He looked like some kind of bad Indiana Jones cosplayer.

He stopped in front of our small group, breathing heavily from the exertion of carrying all that crap. "Sorry, I was running a bit behind this morning. So much to pack," he said, dabbing at the sweat beading on his forehead with a red kerchief.

"You realize we are going to Mexico *City*, right? Not the...jungle?" I asked, waving my hand at his get-up.

"Of course," he said, bushy brows drawing together. "However, for a quest like this, it is best to be fully prepared for anything to happen. There is no telling what we might discover, or what might be required of us."

Swift cleared her throat awkwardly. "We really appreciate you joining us, Professor. This is Sergeant Lopez," she said, gesturing to the other woman. "She is somewhat familiar with Aztec symbolism and mythology. She also grew up in Mexico City and agreed to be our guide."

"Oh, quite pleased to meet you," Gresham said,

eagerly shaking her hand. "Theoretical knowledge of a place is always lacking. It's wonderful to have a local's perspective."

Lopez shook his hand in a daze, throwing a weak glare my way.

I smirked at her as the train we needed pulled into the station. "We should get on before it gets too crowded," I said, ushering the group forward.

Gresham nodded. "Of course, though I don't mind standing. It feels rather good to be stretching my legs. I don't get out of the bookstore as often as I should."

Swift and I exchanged a look as we fell into step behind him, both struggling to suppress our laughter.

"Did you two idiots plan this?" Lopez demanded in a whisper.

Swift clamped her hand across her mouth to hold in the laughter and shook her head vehemently.

"You can't fault him for wanting to be prepared, now can you?" I said, putting my arm around Lopez's shoulders.

"If my mother finds out, I will sacrifice you to whatever Aztec deity I need to in order to appease her," Lopez bit out, elbowing me in the side.

I grunted in pain and removed my arm. "Noted."

Swift lost her struggle to contain her mirth and snorted.

"You too," Lopez said, turning her glare on Swift, whose shoulders were now shaking in silent laughter.

If Lopez's mother was anything like her daughter, her wrath was probably terrifying, but I couldn't take anything seriously while watching Gresham try to fit through the door to the Rune Rail with that backpack on. He finally crouched down and half crawled inside, then looked back at us with a triumphant expression.

This was going to be an...interesting trip.

THIRTY-ONE

I usually felt underdressed without a suit, but under the hot, midday sun I was glad to be wearing a loose shirt. Lopez and I had taken a bus from our downtown hotel to Colonia Roma, a district within the sprawling city that seemed to never end. Mexico City boasted the largest metropolitan area in the western hemisphere, edging out New York City by a measly one and a half million people.

Swift and Gresham were headed to some university library to speak with one of her old coworkers from Magical Artifacts. Splitting up had seemed like the best option to cover more ground in our limited time.

"You're fluent in Spanish, right?" Lopez asked as we turned down a long street lined with restaurants, bars, and shops.

"Yeah, but it's not my best language. I understand it

much better than I can speak it. My accent is awful," I said. My mouth watered as the smell of food drifted toward us.

Mexico City, like all the other major cities, had flourished after the Rune Rail was opened. Tourism had grown, but it was the influx of new jobs that had changed the city the most. Everywhere you went, you saw the mix of magic with human technology. The buildings were sturdier, reinforced with runetech to withstand earthquakes. The once-polluted air was as fresh and clean as you'd find on a mountain top thanks to the special wind turbines installed in the high-rises.

But we weren't here as tourists. It was an odd location for it, but the local IMIB office was smack dab in the middle of one of the hippest neighborhoods in the city. We hadn't given the agent in charge here any warning we were coming. People's reactions to unexpected visits often told you more than anything else. I hoped they weren't involved with the warlock, but anything was possible.

"Here it is," Lopez said as we walked up to a ten-story tall building that looked completely out of place between the French-style mansions that stood on either side. No one lived in the old houses anymore since they'd all been converted to shops. The IMIB office was the only new construction in the area.

I sighed in relief as we walked into the air conditioned building. The atrium was tall and brightly lit, but the dark wood still made it seem oppressive. Lopez walked toward the front desk and nodded at the agent that greeted us.

"I'm Sergeant Lopez, and this is Detective Blackwell," she said, pulling out her badge. "We're here to speak with Detective Juarez."

"Did you have an appointment?" the agent asked, picking up her phone.

"No, but we're old friends," Lopez said with a smile. "He'll know who I am."

The agent took just a couple of minutes to confirm our information, then directed us to the top floor. We walked over to the elevators, and Lopez selected floor six.

"Old friends?" I asked, raising my eyebrow.

Lopez shrugged. "We dated for a couple of months, nothing serious. He got promoted to detective, and my application to be transferred to Moira was finally accepted. It was an amicable split. I think he helped push my application through, actually. He knew the opportunity meant a lot to me."

"How honest do you think we can be with him?"

She pursed her lips. "I'd like to think he is trustworthy, but I'm not willing to stake the investigation on it. It's been a couple of years since we've even spoken. A lot could have happened in that time."

The elevator dinged and the doors slid open. "Fair enough, I'll follow your lead."

We were halfway down the hall when a door near the end opened. A man with trendy black hair and a full beard stepped out. "Lopez," he greeted with a grin, giving me a curious look. "I wasn't expecting to see you back in this old building for at least a decade. You aren't transferring back, are you?"

"Hell no," Lopez said with a laugh. "I'm here with this sucker on a case." She jabbed her thumb at me.

"Detective Alejandro Juarez, but feel free to call me Alejandro. We don't stand on ceremony around here," he said, extending his hand to me.

"Detective Logan Blackwell," I said, shaking his hand firmly. "Everyone calls me Blackwell." The only people that had ever called me Logan were my parents, Hiroji, and a couple of girlfriends. I preferred to keep it that way.

"Come in," he said, waving us toward his office. "Can I get you coffee, or anything else to drink?"

We both declined the offer. His office had a good view of the area. As this was the tallest building on the street, I could see over the roofs of the surrounding structures.

We took the chairs across from him while he sat down behind his desk, the picture of ease. "What case brings you all the way out here?"

"The warlock," Lopez said with a meaningful look.

Alejandro's face hardened, and the sense of ease vanished. "Is he targeting Mexico City next?"

If the man was putting on an act, it was a damn good one. The concern appeared very real.

"Most likely not, but we have information that leads us to believe he has been here multiple times over the past couple of years. He may have even been living in the city at one point," I said, watching his reaction carefully.

His frown deepened. He hadn't known any of this.

Lopez leaned forward. "Could he be getting in and out of the city unnoticed, without traveling through Moira or a border checkpoint?"

"Definitely. There's a man named Juan Carlos Perez you should speak with about that. On the surface, he's an importer. In reality, he's a smuggler. We haven't been able to get any solid evidence on him, but his reputation is well-known," Alejandro said, staring off into the distance as he thought.

He sat up abruptly and pulled open his desk drawer, taking out a notepad. "I'll write down a few names and addresses for you."

"Will he talk to us?" Lopez asked.

Alejandro snorted. "He'll talk your ear off. Juan Carlos likes to *entertain*."

"Have any Aztec artifacts gone missing recently?" I asked as he jotted down the information.

Pausing, he looked up. "There was a museum robbed almost six months ago. We never found a single lead."

"Was magic used in the robbery?"

Alejandro nodded. "Magic was used to kill two guards, as well as a cleaning woman. It was completely unnecessary violence."

"Which museum? I'd like to talk to them as well," Lopez said.

"I'll add them to the list." He hesitated, tapping his pencil against the notepad. "Your question about Aztec artifacts has brought something else to mind. A series of temples have reopened in the boroughs. I hadn't thought anything of it before now. It certainly didn't seem like it was connected to a warlock in any way, but you seem to think he's after something related to them."

I curled my hand into a fist. This god, or whatever it was, was okay with a warlock killing in its name. Every temple should be ripped down.

"The ritual magic he's been using contains Aztec symbols. He's been taking the hearts of mages and sacrificing them," Lopez explained, disgust clear on her face.

Alejandro finished his list and passed it to Lopez. "I'm going to look into recent murders. If anyone has been killed in a similar way, I'll let you know. Is your phone number still the same?"

Lopez nodded and stood. "Thanks for your help, Alejandro."

"Anytime. A warlock is bad news for everyone. I'll do whatever I can to help you catch him faster. I don't like that he's been in my city without my noticing," Alejandro said, clenching his jaw tightly. He walked us to the door, shaking my hand and giving Lopez a quick hug. "Stay safe out there."

"We'll talk again soon," Lopez said, with a smile.

Alejandro shut the door to his office behind him, and we headed back to the elevator.

"I'll send the museum information to Swift since she and Gresham are close by, but I think we should go talk to the smuggler," I said as we waited.

"Agreed. I doubt he'll be up front with us, but what he doesn't say should be just as informative," Lopez said. "Who knows, maybe we can buy our answers. Money talks with guys like him."

Samuel Costa was slippery, but we were getting closer to catching him. We just had to figure out what he wanted in order to stop him.

THIRTY-TWO

A car honked right behind us as a pedestrian began crossing the street without bothering to look at the light. This was one city I was glad I wasn't driving in. The pedestrians acted like they were invincible, and the drivers were aggressive. I could deal with the latter, but the combination of the two wasn't ideal.

"Here it is," Lopez announced, pointing at a quaint and inviting little cafe. Pots with little pink flowers hung in the windows, and laughter drifted toward us on the breeze.

I stopped in my tracks, nonplussed.

"What's wrong?" Lopez asked, nose twitching as she scented the area for danger.

"I expected some kind of shady warehouse, not a cafe in historic Mexico City with what smells like...cinnamon?"

Lopez laughed. "It's churros. And he wouldn't be a very good criminal if he made it obvious, now would he?"

"Indeed I would not," a man said, walking up behind us.

Juan Carlos wasn't as old as I expected. In fact, nothing about him was what you'd expect. His western style cowboy suit was embroidered with intricate designs that should have looked old-fashioned, but the cut made it modern. He had a sleek handlebar mustache and a goatee. A curl of dark brown hair hung down on his forehead. He stopped in front of us, smiling cheekily at Lopez. "How can I help you, agents?"

"I'd like a churro and some coffee, but we do also have a couple of questions," I said, drawing his attention.

"Good choice! Business is always better with food involved. Follow me," he said, waving us inside.

It was still a bit hot to be comfortable inside the building, but the ceiling fans were on full blast, cooling the sweat on my skin. Juan Carlos led us toward the back, pausing only to give instructions to a waitress. He made a show of pulling out Lopez's seat, then settled himself across from us.

"Nice place you have here," I said, looking around. Regardless of whatever else he might do behind the scenes, the cafe was a legitimate and popular business.

"Thank you. My mother worked hard to start this

business, and I am happy to carry on her legacy," he said with a bright grin.

A waitress arrived carrying a tray with three steaming hot coffees and a small basket of churros. My mouth watered in anticipation. I didn't get to this area often, and I'd forgotten how good the food was.

"Your partner, the one with the pink hair, has been running around to all the museums, asking questions," Juan Carlos said, grabbing a churro for himself. He took a bite, crunching loudly, then spoke around a mouthful of food. "I'm almost surprised to see the two of you here."

I swallowed my own bite before speaking, since I possessed actual manners. "How do you know any of that? We didn't announce our trip here."

"I have eyes and ears all over. IMIB agents showing up is a good thing to know, even though I run perfectly legitimate businesses." The smirk on his face made it clear the opposite was true, but we weren't here about a smuggling case.

"We heard you knew a little bit about everything. Have you ever seen this man?" Lopez asked, pulling up a picture of Costa.

His whole demeanor changed. He smacked her hand down, hiding the photo from view. He leaned in, sweat glistening on his forehead in the dim lighting. "I'll answer your questions, then I'm leaving. Don't come back, and don't talk to my people, or you will get them killed."

"You're scared of Costa?" I asked, not expecting such an extreme reaction.

"If that's the man in the picture, then yes," he hissed, angry. "Maybe you should just leave now."

"We will, *after* you answer our questions," I said, grabbing his arm before he could bolt. "Is Costa in the city now?"

"No, but he comes back at least once a month. The old priest is insane. The only reason I'm still alive is because I'm human," he said, eyes darting around like someone might jump out at any moment. "He's only been killing mages, like you."

"How many has he killed?"

"I don't know." Juan Carlos shook his head. "Your kind calls him a warlock, but that's not what he is. He's a fanatic. I took on the first job thinking it was easy money, but I've been forced to work for him for *nothing* ever since. He's already killed three of my men, and I know he'll kill me eventually just because I know too much. Now that you've shown up at my doorstep, I'm fucked."

"We can protect you," Lopez said, but Juan Carlos was already shaking his head.

"No offense, but he's one of you. I'd rather take my chances with my own people. The plans have already been made. I was just waiting until the last moment to disappear. You've just decided the day for me."

"Can you tell us anything about him, or where he might be?" I asked. "We're going to stop him."

Juan Carlos smoothed his fingers over his mustache, clearly nervous. "Outside of the city, near the old Aztec temples, there is a hidden entrance to *something*. I've never been inside, but I've delivered...things...to him there. I don't know what he's doing out there, but it's not good."

"Could you point it out on a map?" I asked.

"I'll do you one better," he said, pulling a folded piece of paper out of his back pocket. "This will lead you to it. Now, please go. I don't know anything else about the crazy old priest."

It was clear that he was too scared to say any more. I couldn't blame him. A prosaic was no match for a super-natural, especially this warlock. Even Swift and I had barely been able to injure him. Costa could snuff out Juan Carlos' life with barely a thought.

Lopez grabbed his hand and shoved her card into it. "If you change your mind, call me."

He nodded and shooed us away from the table, but Lopez and I both knew he'd never call. As we stepped back out into the heat, my phone buzzed with a message from Swift. She'd found something and wanted to meet back at the hotel. I quickly texted that we were on our way.

"Swift and Gresham found something. I let her know we'd head back to the hotel," I said, slipping my phone back in my pocket.

Lopez nodded in acknowledgement. "He was terrified of Costa."

"He probably should be. Costa has been operating under everyone's noses for almost two years, and the IMIB is just now showing up and asking questions. The whole organization looks incompetent," I said, anger leaking into my tone. The IMIB was a necessary thing, but the different magical races still maintained so much power. Too much. They protected their own when they shouldn't, and most of their self-policing was just to prevent scandals. Things like this highlighted the flaws of allowing stuff like that to continue.

"We need to catch this guy soon," Lopez said, shaking her head as we walked down the crowded street.

I nodded in agreement. Every day he was free, there was a chance another innocent person would die. Hopefully, this map would give us the key to finding him.

THIRTY-THREE

I put my keycard in the lock, but the door was yanked
open. Swift beckoned us inside, excitement evident
on her face.

"We found something," she said, holding up a picture
of an old stone with a symbol carved into it.

The design was exactly the same as the amulet Costa
had used to drain some of my magic. "There's a reason
this didn't seem to fit in with anything else. Half the
symbolism on the altar was Greek, half Aztec. This is
neither. It's Egyptian."

"Egyptian? That's a strange combination of religions," I said, furrowing my brow.

"There's no way he did that by accident," Lopez said
with a frown. "The smuggler said he was a fanatic. Why
would he be mixing things like that? Wouldn't that be
blasphemy?"

"Just wait, it gets better," Gresham said, rubbing his hands together eagerly.

"The symbols indicate it has something to do with the Egyptian god of chaos, Apep. Which, at first, threw us off. However, on the altar the Aztec references point to a god called Tezcatlipoca, who was associated with many things including discord, war, and strife. And the Greek symbols point to Ares. Another god of war and chaos. They're all connected, like different faces of the same deity," she said, pointing out each of the symbols on a picture of the altar in turn.

"There are some theories that all religions worship the same gods. A blatant example is the Romans. They simply took the Greek deities and renamed them," Gresham said, adjusting his glasses. "Aphrodite became Venus, and Ares became Mars."

"My theory is that, to this warlock, they're all one and the same. And this," she said, holding up the picture of the device again, "is somehow gathering a sacrifice. At some point he's going to present an offering to this...combined deity. The common thread in all of these deities is chaos, or violence. Every attack by the warlock has been, well, violent and chaotic."

This was Swift in her element. Her experience with Magical Artifacts was priceless on this case. I knew I'd have been lost without her.

"Do you know how the amulet works? Can we disable it?" I asked.

"Not yet, but it's a start. Something about it seems familiar, like I've seen it somewhere."

"We found something too," I said, handing her the map. "Maybe we'll find your answers there."

She scanned the map, then looked up, confused. "What is this, exactly?"

"A smuggler that worked for Costa said this is where he's been going when he visits Mexico City," I said, tapping on the little red X that marked the hidden entrance.

"If we leave early tomorrow morning, we could make it there before lunch," Lopez said.

"Any chance Costa will be there?" Swift asked, glancing at Gresham.

I shrugged. "The smuggler didn't seem to think he was in town, but it's possible. Professor, it might be safer for you to stay behind."

"Oh, heavens no!" he exclaimed. "I'm not so feeble that I couldn't keep myself together during a fight. I was an infantryman during the Mage Wars, you know."

"Really?" Swift asked, looking surprised. "I thought druids were all pacifists."

"Only the prissy ones," he said, waving his hand at her. "I don't believe in standing around philosophizing when there is a war on."

"Alright, it's your choice," I said with a shrug.

Gresham and Swift went over to a side table to study the map and decide the best route to take.

Lopez pulled me aside and crossed her arms, giving me a severe look that was at odds with her soft features. "I know there's something you aren't sharing with me. I get it, sometimes you have to play it close to the chest. But when you two get ready to take on the Mage's Guild, you better tell me."

"What makes you think we're going to do that?" I asked, glancing at Swift. She was apparently still listening and caught my eye, shaking her head slightly to tell me she hadn't said anything.

"Neither of you can stand people getting away with things they shouldn't," Lopez said, nodding at each of us. "You always do the right thing, even when it's likely to get you killed. Combining the two of you was like taping nitro to a jackhammer. That shit's going to blow, and when it does, it's taking down everything around it."

"I've sworn off blowing things up," I said with a smile, attempting to lighten the conversation a little.

"I don't believe that for a second," Lopez said with a roll of her eyes. "Just tell me before you make your move. I want to help."

After a moment's hesitation, I nodded. We couldn't afford to turn down allies, not with gods getting involved. I trusted Lopez, too. She was good people.

THIRTY-FOUR

A mosquito buzzed around my head. I swatted at it angrily. They'd already gotten me a few times, and my neck itched like crazy. They were nasty, vile, blood-sucking parasites that should be exterminated from the face of the earth.

Swift brushed the vines away from a section of the stone. "I think we found it. This is the symbol on your map," she said, tracing the engraving with her finger.

"Thank god," I muttered in relief. Tromping through the jungle was not my idea of a pleasant morning.

"Doesn't look much like a door," Lopez said, walking a little further down. "Maybe it's on the other side."

"Wait," Swift said. Holding her finger about an inch away from the stone, she traced a rune in the air that matched the symbol exactly. The bright orange magic sunk into it. The whole structure shuddered briefly, then light poured out of the stone, revealing a doorway two meters tall and one meter wide.

"Get back," I said, pulling her away from it. The door swung outward, narrowly missing her. In front of us was a stairwell that led into impenetrable darkness. Maybe Gresham had the right idea with his Indiana Jones get-up.

"I've just the thing," Gresham announced from behind us. He began digging around in his backpack before pulling something out. "Headlamps!"

"We can just use a lighting orb," I said, as he started pulling more of them out of his giant backpack. "We are mages, after all."

"Terrible idea! We need to be able to sense even the slightest hint of magic. It would muddle everything." He pulled out four prosaic headlamps and passed them around.

I held the awkward contraption and cast a pleading look at Swift, but she was already pulling hers on without complaint. Lopez, at least, looked just as put out as I did.

She handed hers back to Gresham. "I can see in the dark."

"Oh, of course. I quite forgot you were a shifter," he said with a smile, shoving the headlamp back in his pack.

I begrudgingly pulled mine on. It was too tight on

my head, but if we couldn't use *magic* like *normal mages*, then it would have to do.

"I'll go first. Blackwell, you follow me, then Lopez," Swift said, pointing at each of us. "Gresham, you don't mind bringing up the rear, do you?"

"Not at all," he said with a grunt as he struggled to hoist the pack onto his shoulders.

I followed Swift to the entrance. She paused and turned back to me. "Don't touch *anything* while we're down there. You could damage it or set off a booby trap. I'd like to avoid both scenarios."

"It's probably all covered in rat shit and cobwebs, so you don't have to worry about me trying to touch anything. I won't be."

Lopez snorted. "I can confirm the rat shit. It has a very distinct odor."

Swift laughed. "Glad I don't have your nose."

Switching on her headlamp, she began the descent. As I stepped over the threshold, the temperature dropped at least ten degrees. With every step down, the air grew cooler and more humid.

This place must have been around far longer than the warlock. It felt old and abandoned. Dust coated the steps, but it had been recently disturbed. A line ran down the middle where feet had recently walked.

The top of my head scraped the low ceiling, and I hissed in pain, rubbing the scrape.

Swift threw a glare over her shoulder. "I told you not to touch anything."

"That was an accident," I said, gesturing at the ceiling.

"Be careful, then," she said before continuing.

I crouched down a little lower and followed. Rough stone walls lined the narrow stairwell. Something, most likely a spider, scampered away from the light of my headlamp.

I *hated* bugs. Especially spiders. They had too many legs and too many eyes, and some of them jumped. At least they ate mosquitos.

No sunlight reached down this far, but the roots of the trees that grew overhead had burrowed their way through the stone and dirt. They hung down like vines as they sought more soil. I should have worn a hazmat suit down here instead of a headlamp and a t-shirt.

Swift stopped abruptly, and I ran into her back. She reached a hand back to steady me. "There's something odd here."

The stairs had ended, and ahead of us was a narrow hallway. It didn't look much different from the stairwell, but the same sense of warning that must have stopped Swift prickled at the back of my neck.

"A trap?" Gresham asked, standing on his tippy toes to try and see.

"Yes, but one we can get around, I think," Swift said, crouching down to examine it. "The dust is disturbed in a few places, probably from the warlock passing through."

"I can't tell what it does, but it smells faintly of magic," Lopez said, leaning forward and sniffing carefully.

I couldn't smell anything, despite magic having a very distinctive scent similar to ozone. I was glad we'd brought Lopez. We hadn't expected to be navigating our way through traps in an underground tunnel.

"It looks like there are certain places we should step." She lifted her head, and the light of the lamp illuminated the pathway. The floor was made up of square blocks barely large enough to hold a single foot. A clear path wound through them where the warlock's footsteps were visible. Thank god the Aztecs hadn't been big on dusting.

"And if someone slips?" I asked.

"Let's not find out," Swift said as she carefully stepped onto the first stone. She wobbled slightly before regaining her balance.

"Careful," I said, mocking her tone from before.

"Keep it up, and I'll tell them about the arm wrestling." She took the two steps fast, then paused, holding one foot up like a flamingo.

I clamped my mouth shut. That had been humiliating enough when it happened. The story never needed to be repeated.

When she was halfway down she turned her head slightly and waved me forward. "Leave some space between yourselves, but it looks safe so far."

I stepped onto the first stone. It was just small enough that I couldn't set my foot flat. For the first time in my long life, I appreciated Master Hiko's endless lessons on balance.

Silently, I navigated the path. Lopez followed me, moving more quickly than I could. She caught up as I stepped onto a wooden platform that hadn't been visible from the other side. It was just big enough for us all to stand together. It'd be extremely tight once Gresham joined us.

Below us was a pit. There was no ladder, or stairs. Simply darkness.

"Is Gresham coming?" I asked, looking behind Lopez, but I couldn't see him.

"He said he wanted to wait for us all to get through," Lopez said with a shrug.

As if on cue, Gresham came bounding toward us. He was practically running across the stones, skipping nimbly from one to another. Hopping off the final one, he bumped into Lopez, who grabbed him to keep from toppling over.

"How energizing," he said with a grin.

This guy never ceased to surprise me.

"Give me a hand," Swift said, tapping my shoulder. I grabbed her extended hand and held on tightly as she crouched down, then leaned over the edge. She pulled off her headlamp and adjusted the angle of the beam, shining down into the pit. Her fingers tightened around mine. "It's skulls. There must be thousands."

"Human skulls?" I asked, as I pulled her back up, hoping my assumption was wrong.

She nodded.

Lopez tilted her head back and took a deep breath. "It's hard to tell without shifting, but I smell blood, probably human. Some of it might be fresh."

Gresham pulled out a large flashlight and shone the light at the other side of the pit. It illuminated the racks of skulls, which were held on the racks by wooden posts. The racks descended down in steps, with the widest part of the pit at the top.

"Though unfortunately morbid, we can climb down," Gresham said, his earlier enthusiasm dampened by the gruesome sight before us.

Swift nodded, her lips pressed into a thin line, and swung her legs over the edge. As she put her weight on the post, a skull cracked under her feet. She took a deep breath and adjusted, then continued down.

I climbed down after her, careful to step in the same places. The dead couldn't be offended, but it felt disrespectful to callously crush their remains. They should have been buried, not had their skulls strung up on display.

We were all silent until we reached the bottom. I dropped down beside Swift and looked around. The skull racks stretched up about seven meters high all around us. In the center of the pit was an altar, much like the one we'd found in Boston.

Directly behind it, set in the wall and surrounded by skulls, was the stone face of a jaguar. Its mouth was open in a snarl. The eyes were made of black obsidian that had been polished until it was reflective. It made it seem as if the eyes of the jaguar were following us as we walked around the space.

"Do you feel that?" Gresham asked, turning in a circle. "There's magic coming from the altar, of course, but there's something coming from that jaguar head as well."

"The jaguar is the animal counterpart of Tezcatlipoca. It's probably part of the warlock's rituals," Swift said as she walked over to the altar. She pulled out the picture of the device the warlock had used to drain my magic, comparing it to something.

"What did you find?" I asked, walking over.

"This," she said, pointing at a red jewel the size of a walnut sitting amidst the charred remains of the last sacrifice. "I recognize it from my time in Magical Artifacts. We can't destroy it here, but we need to as soon as possible."

"What is it?"

"A source of energy, to put it in the simplest terms. They were used during the war to keep mages going indefinitely during long battles. You know how using magic can wear you out. They were all supposed to be destroyed, but of course they weren't," she said, glaring at the stone as though its existence personally offended her.

I reached for it, but she yanked me back.

"Don't touch it! Are you insane?" she demanded, smacking me on the shoulder.

I rubbed the spot where she hit. "We can't just leave it here. You said it needed to be destroyed."

"I know that, but we have to be careful. It could be booby-trapped."

"Guys, there's something moving in the walls," Lopez said, holding her head close to the skulls rack. "I have a bad feeling about this."

"I agree, we shouldn't linger. We're lucky the warlock wasn't here," Swift said, shaking her head.

"I know exactly how to get the stone safely," Gresham said, approaching the altar.

"I wish we had some time to examine the altar," Swift said, crossing her arms.

"Take some pictures, then we need to get the stone

and get out of here," I said, glancing at Lopez. She was pacing back and forth in a motion I could only describe as prowling. Like a caged animal. Whatever was bothering her was making me nervous as well. I'd never seen her this freaked before.

"What exactly is your plan?" Swift asked Gresham.

He crouched down and stood up with a small rock in his hand. "This looks about the same size. It probably weighs a bit less, but it's the best we can do in the circumstances."

Swift took a step back. "I hope you know what you're doing."

He waved away her concern and positioned himself in front of the altar, knees bent, hands hovering over the stone. "It is simply a matter of nimble reflexes," he quickly switched the bright red stone with the rock, "and confidence," he finished with a grin.

We all stood perfectly still, holding our breath, waiting to see if it had worked. The large stone face of the jaguar stayed dormant, and we breathed a sigh of relief.

"Thank the heavens," Swift said in relief. "That could have been bad."

Gresham tucked the jewel into his backpack. An odd sound got my attention. I turned, searching for the source.

"We should take a few skulls for identification, then call in more agents to—"

"What is that?" I asked, pointing out the sand trickling from the left nostril of the jaguar in a steady stream.

"Shit."

The word sounded wrong coming out of Gresham's mouth, but it spurred everyone into action nonetheless.

THIRTY-FIVE

The jaw of the jaguar fell open, the scrape of stone on stone sounding eerily like a roar. Sand poured out like a river, rushing around our legs. We ran for the walls, scrambling up.

My foot slipped, and sand swept my legs out from under me. Swift grabbed my arm and hauled me up with a grunt, pushing me overhead. I wrapped my hand around a wooden post and yanked her up to my level.

"Go faster!" Lopez shouted. "Whatever is in the walls was being held back by the sand, but it's coming now!"

Gresham passed me and Swift, climbing the walls like a monkey. I lunged up toward the final handhold and pulled myself over the edge, rolling onto the wooden platform. Swift came crawling right after me, reaching back to yank Lopez to the top as well.

"Do you still have the stone?" Swift shouted at Gresham.

"Yes, quickly now!" he shouted.

"Oh my god, it's rats!" Lopez shrieked, elbowing her way past me and Swift. She sprinted into the hallway, hopping from stone to stone.

I made the mistake of looking behind us. The eyes of the jaguar popped out, the obsidian circles hitting the sand. Rats poured from the eye sockets. Thousands of them.

"Go!" I shouted, shoving Swift ahead of me. I extended my left hand behind us and formed a ball of fire. It rushed toward the rats, roasting the first wave. A foul smell filled the room as the nasty vermin shrieked. I hadn't even manage to catch half of them, but it slowed down the wave as the new rats had to crawl over the flaming bodies of their brethren.

"You'll never kill them all. Come on!" Swift yelled over her shoulder.

I turned and raced after her. The entire structure began shaking around us. Dirt and rocks fell from the low ceiling. The rubble hit the pathway, disturbing centuries old dust. Swift coughed, covering her mouth with her shirt. The hair on the back of my neck prickled as magic filled the air.

Flames erupted from the tiles, popping up randomly. This gave a whole new meaning to the-floor-is-lava.

Heat beat against my back as everything crumbled and burned.

"Now would be a good time for ice!" Swift shouted over her shoulder.

I lifted both palms and pushed the magic ahead of us, attempting to smother the flames with ice. Swift ran and jumped onto it, letting her momentum carry her forward like she was surfing. I followed, crouching slightly to maintain my balance, but it was melting quickly. It cracked under my weight, and I was forced to jump.

My feet slipped in the slush, and I hit the ground, rolling in the now disgusting, hot slop of water. A tile cracked underneath me. I quickly rolled to the side, avoiding a burst of flame that still managed to singe my shirt.

Scrambling to my feet, I ran for the stairs. Rats were quickly filling the hall behind us, running across the walls and ceiling to avoid the fire.

The stone began to churn around me, and for a moment, I was sure I was going to be crushed. Then I realized it was Gresham manipulating the stone. The ceiling parted, swallowing up the horde of rats as they continued their reckless charge. The ground rolled under my feet, and I was tossed forward. Swift caught my arm and swung me around to keep me from crashing into the ground. We sprinted free of the tunnel just as it caved in behind us.

Rubble sealed off the exit. A few tendrils of smoke escaped, but everything else was trapped inside.

"That could have gone a bit better," Gresham said, shaking out his arms as though he'd just had a nice little workout.

I couldn't help but laugh at that as I tried to catch my breath. "No kidding, Professor."

THIRTY-SIX

We stepped out of the elevator into the narrow, dimly lit hall. Two lights were out this time, shrouding the end of the hallway in darkness.

Gresham and Swift had destroyed the stone we had taken from Mexico City as soon as we'd arrived back in Moira. We'd all gotten a solid night's sleep as well. Now, armed with more information, it was time to talk to my favorite IMIB employee.

"Just be polite, and Patrice is sure to love you," I said, patting Swift on the shoulder.

"I'm always polite," Swift said with a frown.

"Until you get in a fight, then it's all *I'll skin you and wear your flesh as a sundress*," I said, mimicking her voice.

She glared at me. "I'm not responsible for the things I say when I am in a berserker rage."

I laughed at her and opened the door to The Cave.

Patrice was sitting behind her desk, a pen stuck behind her ear. She was the woman to schmooze if you needed something, and today we needed information.

"Patrice, you're looking especially young this morning," I said in greeting.

Her sharp eyes flicked up to me, but a smile played at her lips. She was always happy to see me. "I think I gain ten gray hairs every time you come to visit me. Who is this you have with you?"

I cleared my throat, remembering the reason I last came down here. "Detective Lexi Swift, my partner."

"Ohhhh," Patrice said, her eyes going big. "The mysterious Miss Swift. If you're bringing her down to see me, you must have sorted things out."

"Sorted what out?" Swift asked, immediately suspicious.

"He was trying to figure out who you were, but judging by his guilty expression, he never told you all that." Patrice smiled, shaking her head fondly.

"Oh, I...filled him in on my family situation," Swift said, clearly uncomfortable.

"Communication is important in every relationship," Patrice said, looking at us with a smug expression. "Even a professional one."

"We need information about several people that work for the Mage's Guild," I said, hurrying to change the subject.

"All right, all right, no need to get your panties in a twist," Patrice said, fingers flying over the keyboard. "You have their names?"

"Here," I said, sliding the list Bootstrap had given us through the small slot in the thick, glass barrier. Patrice grabbed it and propped the slip of paper up behind her keyboard.

As she searched each name, a frown formed on her face, deepening her wrinkles. "Did you know half this list was dead?"

"We only suspected one of them might be." Swift shook her head, then looked at me. "I can't believe the Mage's Guild didn't act sooner."

The warlock was killing off his enemies one by one. I was almost certain some of the skulls we had found in Mexico belonged to his dead former coworkers.

Patrice picked up the list and made a little mark next to half the names. "These I'm marking are dead, all within the last year. The remaining people are scattered all over. Every single one of them was relocated or reassigned within the past six months."

David Johnson, the mage whose body Viktor had shown us, was marked as dead. Costa must be using his former coworkers as sacrifices.

"Do any of them work in Moira?" I asked.

"Sure, two of them are in Moira now, actually. One is in New York City, and another is in Boston. The last is in Tokyo." Patrice handed the paper back through the slot. "I can send you their contact information."

"Please do," Swift said.

New York. Boston. All the places the attacks had been. If the trend continued, then Tokyo was at risk. We had to prevent the attack if we could.

THIRTY-SEVEN

"Umm, Mrs. Schmidt is still on that phone call," the secretary said, her eyes twitching toward the door.

We'd been waiting for over ten minutes. Hell, I was starting to wonder if Schmidt was still in her office. I wasn't sure if someone had warned her we were coming, or if she was just too scared to see any kind of visitor. Either way, I was out of patience.

"They'll have to call back," I said, striding past her desk.

"Dammit, Blackwell," Swift muttered as she followed me.

"Sir, you can't just—"

I opened the door, startling a short woman into dropping her purse. She had clearly been gathering her things to leave.

"You must be Mrs. Schmidt," I said, extending my hand. She hesitated between picking up her purse and accepting my handshake, finally deciding on the latter. Her palms were clammy.

"Yes, I am. Who are you?" Her voice trembled almost as much as her hands had.

"I'm Detective Blackwell with the IMIB, and this is my partner, Detective Swift," I said, motioning at Swift.

She stepped forward and shook Mrs. Schmidt's hand as well, smiling apologetically. "Sorry to barge in, but we did need to speak with you as soon as possible."

"I don't see what could be so important," she said, snatching her purse off the floor and straightening her shoulders. "None of my work overlaps with the IMIB."

"You worked with Samuel Costa a couple of years ago, didn't you?" Swift asked, looking around the office. There were an alarming number of knick-knacks on the cluttered shelves that lined the walls.

Mrs. Schmidt's fingers went white-knuckled where she gripped the purse strap. "Costa? Sure, but he died two years ago. Right after that I was finally transferred here, to Moira."

"Who told you he died?" I asked.

"I don't...I don't know. We were just told, and then everyone was transferred."

"You'll be happy to know that he's actually alive and

well," I said, slipping my hands into my pockets and smiling at her.

Her mouth dropped open and she wheezed, apparently incapable of words.

"Or not."

"Did you know Costa well?" Swift asked.

"No," she replied angrily before practically running for the door. "I have an appointment I have to get to."

"Mrs. Schmidt we really need to—"

"No!" she screeched, pausing to look at us with wide eyes. "Just — no." She turned and hurried out of the office. "Katie, I won't be back today. Cancel all my meetings."

Swift looked at me. "She really thought he was dead."

"And now she's terrified. She expects him to come for her," I said, rubbing my hand along my jaw.

THIRTY-EIGHT

We had chased down every single still-living coworker that had been transferred to Moira. All of them were terrified of Costa, and most had thought he was dead. A few seemed to have suspected otherwise, and they were the most scared out of all of them.

The coworker based in Tokyo hadn't been at work or at home, and no one knew where he hung out. I'd sent a message to Bootstrap asking the runehacker to track him down.

"He could be dead already," Swift said as we walked into my apartment.

"He killed all his other coworkers right before an attack. I doubt he'd change his M.O. now, especially since it might be part of some ritual."

The door opened behind Swift, and Yui strolled in. Without saying a word, she walked past me and grabbed a soda out of the refrigerator.

"Where have you been?" I asked.

She popped the tab open and took a sip. "Around. Why, were you worried?"

"Actually, yes," I said angrily. "You see, we had a weird visitor the other day. It claimed to be a god."

"People are always claiming to be gods," Yui said with a derisive sniff. "Some people even worship kitsune as deities, you know."

"You knew the god was coming, didn't you?" Swift asked, crossing her arms.

"That sounds more like an accusation than a question." Yui narrowed her green eyes at Swift.

"Deflecting questions instead of answering them is often a sign of guilt." Swift put her hands on her hips and raised her eyebrow in my direction.

I pinched the bridge of my nose between my thumb and forefinger. "Yui, what do you know about Fate?"

Her nose twitched and she averted her eyes. "I don't put much stock in ideas like fate or destiny, personally."

"You know what I'm asking, stop avoiding the question," I snapped, losing all patience. "That creature, whatever it was, showed up in my apartment and did things that should be impossible. And my *guardian* was nowhere to be seen."

"Then there was nothing to guard you against. I must do everything in my power to keep you alive, but that doesn't mean I have to show up to keep you from being inconvenienced," Yui said, crossing her arms.

"*Inconvenienced?*" Swift demanded, pink smoke leaking from her eyes as she became enraged.

"You're both being childish," Yui said with a growl. Her features flickered between fox and human. "Instead of wondering where I was, maybe ask why Fate was here. Ask yourself why a *god* would possibly be interested in either of you. Ask what's coming next."

I stood in shock for a moment. Yui had dropped the pouty ingenue persona, and it was a little scary. It was easy to forget she was a powerful supernatural creature when she was shedding on my sheets and leaving crumbs on the couch. It was easy to forget she was a trickster.

"Why was Fate here?" Swift asked through clenched teeth.

"Certainly not because he needed your help," Yui said, rolling her eyes.

"Fate is real, is this other god real? The one the warlock worships?" I asked.

"They're all real, aren't they? Every single deity that's ever been worshipped," Swift added.

Yui snorted. "Not *every* single one, but most are."

"Can they be killed?" I asked.

Fate had been able to move us around without so much as blinking. He'd masqueraded as people I knew, and it had been impossible to tell the difference. He'd been inside my head. Something that powerful was terrifying.

The kitsune looked at me. "That's a dangerous question. They would say no."

"What would you say?" I knew I wouldn't get a straight answer, but I needed to see her reaction.

"That you shouldn't even ask." Yui took another drink then crumpled the empty can and tossed it in the trash. She wouldn't meet my eyes. I wasn't sure if that meant the answer was yes or no, but it did mean the question scared her.

"You mentioned something else was coming. What is it?" Swift asked.

"This warlock, do you think he was visited by a god? Told he had a purpose?" Yui asked, walking toward Swift. "Do you think he was given gifts? Power?"

"Yes," Swift said, her face going contemplative. She looked back up, her eyes wide. "They're choosing soldiers."

I didn't like the sound of that. "Soldiers?"

"This god of war and destruction chooses a warlock to carry out these sacrifices. Fate chooses you. These attacks must be tests, just the first moves in a war," Swift said, speaking so rapidly I almost couldn't keep up. She turned, pacing up and down the living room. "This isn't even a real battle. It's a precursor."

"Bingo," Yui said.

THIRTY-NINE

"Blackwell! Swift! My office, now!" Bradley shouted as soon as we stepped off the elevator.

"What did you blow up this time?" Zang asked, leaning back in his chair and resting his hands behind his head. I'm sure he was eager for popcorn and another video showing up of us stumbling around like idiots. Too bad he was going to be disappointed.

"Your mom!" Swift shouted back, striding to Bradley's office with her head held high. The office erupted into laughter behind us, except for Zang who was left red-faced.

I opened the door for Swift, waving her inside ahead of me. For a brief second, I thought about slamming the door shut and making a run for it, leaving her to deal with Bradley...but she'd hunt me down if he didn't. With a sigh, I walked in and sat down across from Mr. Shouty.

He was turned away from us in his chair, muttering something. His hairy hand reached out and grabbed the edge of his desk, pulling himself around slowly. He smoothed down his mustache and adjusted his tie to lay flat on his wide stomach. Then, finally, looked at us.

"Troublemakers. That's what you are. *Both* of you. I should have known you'd harass Mage's Guild employees without even warning me, yet I am shocked," he said, his glare settling on Swift for a moment. "My boss wants me to cut you off. Suspend you *indefinitely*. But from your messages, you are also close to solving this case." He leaned back and crossed his hands.

We stared at him silently. This was the glaring part of his rant, and it was not to be interrupted.

"I was able to talk him into giving you forty-eight hours to find, and stop, this warlock," he said finally. "I had to call in a favor for this, so you better not screw it up."

"Forty-eight hours?" Swift repeated, her eye twitching slightly.

"Is that a problem, Detective Swift?" Bradley asked, his mustache bristling in warning.

"Not at all," she said through gritted teeth.

"There's one other thing," Bradley said, shaking his head like he disapproved. "You can't interview any more of Costa's coworkers. That's an order that comes from way over our heads."

Swift dragged her hands through her hair. "That's absolute crap. We have reason to believe they're in danger."

"The Mage's Guild has taken them into protective custody and refuses to discuss the issue further," Bradley said.

"And there's nothing we can do about it, is there?" she asked, her anger growing every second.

"We're close to catching Costa despite that," I said, putting a hand on her shoulder to calm her down. Turning back to Bradley, I continued, "We suspect the next attack will be in Tokyo, and we can be ready for him. We'll need Danner and Lopez for backup, though."

He picked up his latest World's Best Grandad mug and took a long drink. "Do whatever you have to, as long as it works. You fail, and I'll be forced to fire you both. But if you succeed, well, at worst you'll get a couple days of paid...vacation."

Swift stood. "Thank you, sir. We'll get started right away."

I followed her as she practically ran out of his office, her red trench coat billowing behind her. "Hey, wait up," I hissed, jogging to keep up with her fast pace.

"The Mage's Guild is trying to stop us," she said angrily as she stomped forward.

I grabbed her elbow and pulled her to a stop. "Of course they are. This isn't a surprise to either of us."

She turned to face me, pink eyes glowing brightly with restrained rage, and yanked her arm out of my grip. "I know. But I still hate it. It's not right."

"We'll get the warlock, then we'll find out who was covering this up and stop them, too."

She shook her head. "Like we got Bianchi?"

I shoved my hands in my pockets. I knew how she felt. Sometimes it seemed like we were fighting the Mage's Guild as often as we were fighting the bad guys. But giving up wasn't an option. Not for me, at least.

"We'll get him, and we'll stop the corruption in the Mage's Guild. Not today, and probably not tomorrow, but one day. They screwed up with this warlock trying to keep themselves from looking bad."

"What if one day is too far off? I may not even work here in–" She stopped herself and turned away, walking toward our office again.

"Why wouldn't you work here?" I asked quietly as I followed her.

"We'll talk about it after this case," she said as she grabbed the door handle. She stepped through the doorway and paused abruptly. "Lopez, are you okay?"

I stepped around her and found Lopez was sitting in our office, a hard look on her face as she stared at nothing. She shook her head, but didn't respond.

"What happened? Another attack?" I asked.

"Alejandro is dead," she said, her voice as flat as her expression. "Apparently, he went missing yesterday, and what was left of his body turned up this morning, laid out on the steps of the local IMIB office."

My heart dropped into my stomach. We'd gone to see him, but it'd never crossed my mind that the visit would make him a target. "Shit."

Swift put her head in her hands and turned away. Her magic crackled through the air, barely restrained. "I'm sorry we put your friend in danger—"

"Not your fault. Not mine. Not even his. We're going to kill this warlock," she said, turning her dark eyes to us. "Then I'm going to help you take down the people that share equal responsibility for every drop of blood shed. Alejandro wasn't my one true love or some bull-shit like that, but he was a friend, and a good man. He didn't deserve this."

She stood abruptly, every muscle in her body tense, and walked out of the office.

FORTY

"Bradley said we only have forty-eight hours, but I don't think we have even that much time," Swift said, tapping the arm of her chair thoughtfully. "Costa knows we found his altar in Mexico City, he killed Alejandro, and he needs this guy from Tokyo."

"Do you think he'll attack Moira? He does have a few coworkers here."

She thought about it for a second, then shook her head. "Not until he's completed his ritual. That may be his eventual target, though."

I snorted. "If he attacked Moira, it'd make our job easier. The valkyrie would eat him for lunch."

The office door opened, and Danner strolled in. He shut the door firmly behind him, crossed his arms, and glared at us. "Heard this son of a bitch killed one of our own."

I leaned forward and nodded. "He did. Lopez's old friend down in Mexico City."

"You two knuckleheads have a plan for catching this warlock?"

"We're working on one," Swift said, rising from her chair. "It's going to take a small army to stop this guy though. We suspect he's...more powerful than your average evil asshole. You in?"

Danner snorted. "I guess I should come as a chaperone, if nothing else. Whole damn organization is full of kids these days."

Swift turned back to me. "Costa will be looking for this Tokyo employee. We need to find him first."

"Yeah, and that means I need to text our...friend," I said, wiggling my phone at her.

"He better be able to work fast," Swift said, shaking her head.

"The threat of imminent disaster and money tend to motivate him. I'll provide both," I said, as I quickly texted Bootstrap. "We should meet at my apartment in an hour. That way, at least we'll be in Tokyo whenever my contact gets back to me. Danner, can you grab Lopez and bring her?"

He nodded. "Send me your address."

Most of the time, preparing to go capture a bad guy was simple and uneventful. We didn't wear body armor like prosaic cops; our weapons and our protections were inside us already. Our magic was our best chance at winning. Guns or other mundane weapons wouldn't stop a powerful mage or even a shifter.

This case was a pain in the ass, not only because we were facing a warlock, but because the Mage's Guild was so busy trying to keep from being embarrassed that they were making our jobs twice as hard. Bradley had told us to leave Costa's former coworker alone. Unfortunately, we couldn't. Bootstrap was busy tracking him down right now.

"He's taking forever," Swift said, pacing my living room.

Lopez was standing by the door silently, staring at the floor. Usually she would have a snarky comment or even a smile. Instead, she was just tense and angry. I couldn't blame her at all. We were all on edge. Even Danner seemed grumpier than usual.

My phone rang, and everyone flinched. I grabbed it and accepted the call. "Blackwell."

"You're not going to believe this," Bootstrap said with a grin in his voice.

"Try me," I replied through gritted teeth.

"The Mage's Guild has stashed this dude at the High

Chancellor's house in Tokyo, along with a few Magisters."

I looked at Swift in shock and her brows drew together. The last thing this case needed was more interference from the Mage's Guild. I wasn't sure if we'd be able to get to this guy if the Chancellor had him.

"What?" she asked, unable to hear the other side of the conversation.

"Your father has him."

Her face went pale as a sheet, then immediately flushed red. "Which house?"

"The one in Denenchōfu, Ōta Ward," Bootstrap said. I relayed the information to her and she began pacing again.

"This both complicates things and simplifies them," she said, magical energy humming around her.

"I can see how it complicates things, but not how it simplifies them," I said, raising my brow.

She stopped pacing and looked at me. "I can get us in. All of my father's houses have the same emergency exit. If my code doesn't work, we'll figure something out."

"Are we about to break into the Lord High Chancellor's home to find someone the Mage's Guild has put in protective custody?" Lopez asked

"Yes," we said in unison.

She took a deep breath and nodded. "Well, that's one way to die."

"No need to be so pessimistic," Yui said, appearing behind her out of thin air. Lopez jumped and whirled around, growling at the kitsune. Yui bared her teeth right back, her face going foxlike.

"Lopez, wait, she...lives here," I said, cringing at having to admit that.

"You're living with the kitsune now?" Lopez asked, looking horrified.

"More like I can't get her to leave. What are you doing here right now, Yui?"

"You need my help. I'm going with you," Yui said, crossing her arms. I realized that she wasn't wearing her usual kimono. Instead, she wore the traditional armor of an *onna-bugeisha*, or female samurai.

Danner stalked forward. "You play any tricks that might get someone hurt, and I'll cut your tails off and use them to dust my shelves. Got it?"

Yui glared at him. "As if you pose a threat to me."

"Well, that human did manage to steal your ball," Swift said, smirking at her. "Seems like you are pretty vulnerable."

Danner chuckled and headed toward the door. "Let's go give the High Chancellor a kick in the ass and get this warlock put down."

FORTY-ONE

The house turned out to be a three-acre, walled plot of land near downtown Tokyo. The land alone must have been worth a hundred million, if not more. This area of the city was divided up between the rich and powerful. There was a mix of architectural styles, everything from Edwardian villas to Japanese style homes.

We had crept in over the back fence. There wasn't as much security as I expected. Then again, no thief would want to risk breaking into the house of someone this powerful just to steal a television or something equally mundane. Anyone else brazen enough to attack the Chancellor would probably make a big show of it.

Swift crouched in front of a door shimmering with runes. She traced a complicated symbol, but the wards glowed red and began to pulse. "Shit, that should have worked."

"Maybe we should try the front door?" Lopez asked.

"That way has the same wards," Swift said with a shake of her head.

"Time for the backup plan." I pulled out my phone and dialed Bootstrap. Thankfully, he answered immediately. "We need your help."

"You also need to hurry. The warlock is in Tokyo. He'll be at your location within a half hour," Bootstrap said, sounding a little worried.

"Swift thought she could get in the backdoor, but there's some kind of ward and it's not accepting her. Can you runehack it?"

"Turn your camera on and show it to me," he said eagerly.

I activated the video call feature and turned the camera toward the door. "It started pulsing after her last failed attempt."

"Perfect," he said, cracking his knuckles. "Swift, you need to press one hand to the top right corner, then trace a muddling rune in the center. When it starts twisting, just kick the door in."

She turned to glare at the phone. "Are you kidding me? There's no way that'll work."

"Dude, trust me. I'm a genius."

Swift glared at me. I just shrugged. "Want me to try?"

"No," she muttered before smacking her hand against the top right corner. She angrily traced the rune he'd specified. Immediately, the whole thing began pulsing faster. The door began to glow behind the writhing magic. With a crack, the bright lines all twisted together.

"Now!" Bootstrap shouted from the phone.

She lifted her foot and kicked inward, smashing through the ward and the door. The door was ripped off its hinges and flew down the hallway.

"Well, damn. It actually worked," Lopez said, looking surprised. "Who is this kid?"

"I'm not a kid, I'm nineteen," Bootstrap shouted angrily. "Now, you have about twenty-eight minutes left. Hurry up, and try not to die. You're a good customer, Blackwell."

"Glad to hear you're concerned for me," I muttered before hanging up the phone. Swift was still standing in the doorway, looking murderous. I stepped up beside her. "You ready to do this?"

She nodded. "Yeah, let's get it over with."

Staticky magic prickled along the back of my neck as we walked over the threshold. Runehacking wasn't popular. Most people thought it was a cheap trick. There were only a few people in the world that really knew what they were doing with it. Lucky for us, Bootstrap was one of them.

Looking around as we walked, I wondered how

Swift had turned out like she did. She had to have grown up spoiled; even this escape tunnel was luxurious. The walls were smooth, and the floor was impeccably clean. Soft, recessed LEDs lit our path. The tunnel was straight and led upward, but not so steeply that it made the walk strenuous. She hadn't, though. That took strength of character most people didn't have, or some kind of life changing experience.

At the end of the tunnel was a door. A screen above it showed the room we'd be entering. It was a library of some sort. In the center of the room, a man was pacing. Every few moments, he tugged at his hair or scratched his arm.

There were three guards with him, all dressed in the black robes of a magister.

"Three magisters?" Lopez whispered. "They're serious about protecting this guy."

"They're serious about not being embarrassed," Swift said as she leaned over to inspect the door. She typed a code into the electronic pad, and it beeped green. Guess they thought changing the outside wards would be enough to keep her out and hadn't changed all the codes.

She grabbed the handle. "I'll go in first. They should

recognize me. We don't really want to have to fight them as well as the warlock."

I nodded and stepped up behind her. "Fine, but if they attack, I'm going to blast them away."

Lopez and Danner stood flat against the wall, ready to go. Taking a deep breath, she turned the handle and pushed the door open. It swung outward, and the man in the center of the room shrieked like he'd been stabbed and dropped to the floor, whacking an end table with his elbow. A glass bowl of red marbles fell, shattering as it hit the floor. The marbles scattered in every direction, along with the tiny shards of glass.

The magisters turned to face us, clearly startled.

Swift walked in, hands held high. "I'm Detective Lexi...Alexis Swift, and I need to speak with this man."

The Magister to her right snorted. "He is under the protection of the Mage's Guild. You've overstepped your authority as an IMIB agent by breaking into the Lord High Chancellor's personal home."

"I'm his daughter. It's hardly breaking and entering," she snapped back.

"His *disgraced* daughter," the magister corrected.

She ground her teeth together. "The warlock, Samuel

Costa, is on his way here right now. This house's defenses will not be enough to stop him."

The magister's eyes narrowed. "How do you know that? We took every precaution when bringing Mr. Miller here."

"Yet, we still found him," I said, stepping around Swift to stand next to her. "Costa is on his way, and if you want this guy to live, I suggest taking him elsewhere."

The magister turned away and motioned for his colleagues to join him. They cast a rune to block the sound while they spoke.

Lopez and Danner crept out behind us.

"This isn't a good room to face this warlock. Is there a courtyard outside?" Danner asked, looking around.

"Yeah, there are two, but the warlock will be expecting them to be holding Miller inside," Swift said.

The magister turned back around abruptly and pulled out a phone. He dialed a number while glaring at Swift. "Since this is the Lord High Chancellor's decision, we will consult him before deciding."

Swift's teeth ground together so hard I could hear it. I squeezed her shoulder, but she shrugged my hand off. I guess now was not the time to be sympathetic.

The magister had a quiet conversation with the Chancellor before turning to Swift. "He wants to talk to you."

Well, shit. After the threats he'd made to me, this wasn't exactly how I'd hoped this would go.

She walked over, snatched the phone away from the magister, and put it to her ear. "Yes, Father?"

She stood perfectly still while he spoke, not responding, and not giving any hint as to how the conversation was going. After a few moments, she quietly answered, "No," then handed the phone back to the magister.

He took the phone with a smug look that quickly fell off his face as he listened to his new instructions. His fingers tightened on the phone. "Yes, Lord Chancellor."

She turned back to face us, her face crimson with anger and her eyes flashing. "They're going to leave and take Miller somewhere safer. If the warlock isn't dealt with by morning...well...let's just make sure he's dead."

FORTY-TWO

It was pitch black outside. The tiny sliver of the moon was barely visible through the window but shed no light on the courtyard this room overlooked. Even the clouds were dark, threatening rain. A sense of doom had settled in my chest. I was alone in the room. Waiting. Pacing. Swift had cast an illusion to shroud my face, and it made my skin itch.

Thunder rumbled in the distance, and I jerked. Sighing, I dragged my hand down my face. I was as jumpy as a Chihuahua. Patience was not one of my virtues on a good day, and today definitely wasn't good.

The sky opened up and rain poured down, obscuring my already limited view. The wind picked up, and the whole house groaned under the onslaught. Frowning, I stood by the window. This seemed more like a cyclone than a thunderstorm.

A footstep scuffed against the floor, and a cold wind rushed past me. He was here.

I tensed and slowly turned to face the intruder.

Shrouded in smoke and a dark cape, Costa stood before me. "I saved you for last, Edgar," he said, pushing the hood back to reveal his face. There were dark circles beneath his eyes, as though he hadn't slept in days. "I promised you when I left the Mage's Guild that one day I would rip your still-beating heart from your chest."

"Did you really?" I asked. Standing in front of him right now, it was almost hard to believe all the things he'd done. He was just a man, but when you looked into his eyes, you saw the dark power lurking inside him. Power he never should have had.

The vicious grin on Costa's face faltered. "Who are you?"

With a quick twist of my fingers, the illusion fell away. I grinned. "Surprise, motherfucker."

"Blackwell," he growled, as rage spread across his features. He glanced around as though expecting to see Edgar trembling in a corner. "Where is he?"

"No clue," I said with a shrug. "But it doesn't matter. You aren't leaving this place alive."

He cackled and the sound sent chills down my spine. "Did you come here alone to stop me?"

"Of course not. I'm not stupid," I said, taking a step

back. That was supposed to be the cue, but nothing happened. I took another step back.

Costa's grin returned and a red glow started behind his eyes. "It doesn't matter how many friends you brought with you tonight. They can all join you as sacrifices."

He lifted his hand toward me and the amulet hanging around his neck twitched. I wasn't going to wait for that thing to get a hold on me again. Throwing caution to the wind, I leaped over the couch, hitting the ground with a roll and grabbing my katana. Magic blasted the spot where I had been standing, shattering the window and sending chunks of marble flying through the air.

I drew the black blade as I twisted around, slicing through the next attack. Costa pressed both palms together, preparing another spell. He stumbled forward with a grunt as Lopez hit his back in her panther form.

She clamped her jaws around the back of his robes and yanked backward. Danner ran in from the left and Swift from the right. We had one surprise attack, and this was it.

Danner cast a fire spell that engulfed Costa. Lopez leaped away just in time, sliding to a stop a few feet away. The warlock bellowed in pain, and Swift lifted her mace overhead, swinging it down with a shout. I charged in, ready to finish him off if Swift's attack didn't kill him, but as her mace landed, a sudden wave of dark magic exploded outward.

It lifted me from my feet and threw me through the air like I weighed nothing. I reached for the shield rune on my katana, but I slammed into a bookcase before I could do anything. Stars exploded behind my eyes as my head snapped backward and I hit the floor.

With a groan, I rolled onto my knees. In the center of the room, a bubble of pure darkness sat where Costa had been. It pulsed like a heartbeat. I couldn't see Danner or Lopez anywhere, but Swift was crawling back in through a broken window, shaking glass from her hair.

"What the hell is that?" My voice sounded oddly muffled since my ears were still ringing from the explosion.

"I don't know," she said, her eyes blazing with anger. "But I'm going to crush it."

"I don't think—"

She charged in without any regard for my warning. Her mace rebounded off the bubble, and a flare of magic threw her back for a second time. Twisting in the air, she managed to land on her feet.

Danner ran in from the opposite side, fire pouring from his hands. It hit the edge of the darkness and surged around it, unable to penetrate the strange magic.

"Does anyone see Lopez?" I shouted over the chaos.

There was an angry hiss, and I spotted her struggling out from under a collapsed section of the wall. She was limping but didn't look any worse off than the rest of us.

Movement in my peripheral vision startled me, and I whipped around. Yui hopped up onto the ledge of the window, broken glass crunching under her feet. Her hair whipped around her and her eyes glowed a brilliant yellow. It was about time she started helping.

"Does this mean I'm about to die?" I asked, edging closer to her and Swift.

She turned to me. "Perhaps. He is transforming into the vessel of his god."

That did not sound good. "Can we stop it?"

"Probably not."

Well, that wasn't a no. And I wasn't going to stand around and wait for him to transform.

"With me!" I shouted at Swift. She nodded and we charged in together. Our weapons collided with the dark magic simultaneously. The impact jarred my arm and shoulder painfully but didn't even crack the damn thing. It had stopped growing, but the feeling of magic in the air was only growing thicker.

There was a flash of light behind us as Yui transformed into a huge white kitsune. The wall gave way to her mass, crumbling into a pile of rubble around her feet. I wasn't sure if it was my imagination, but she looked bigger than last time. Her two red-tipped tails writhed behind her, and the air around her grew hot with magic.

She bared her teeth and let out a shriek that made my eardrums hurt all over again. The dark thing began to vibrate with the sound of her voice. The walls rattled, and the floor shook beneath our feet.

"I don't think that's a good sign," Swift shouted over the racket.

"I second that!" Danner said, backing away.

I grabbed Swift and jerked her backward, throwing up a shield one-handed with the katana. The bubble cracked violently, then exploded upward with such force the upper floors and roof were completely blown away. Wind and rain pelted the shield, along with chunks of the house. I gritted my teeth against the onslaught, holding it up through sheer force of will.

The darkness blew away on the wind like smoke, revealing something out of my nightmares. The warlock still stood in the rubble, but extending from him like a shadow, and towering over us, was a skeleton wreathed in black flame. The hollow eyes looked down upon us, burning with hate.

"I will strip the flesh from your bones and mount your skulls in my temple," Costa's voice boomed, echoing through the demolished house. It seemed to come from him and the skeleton simultaneously.

It lifted one huge arm and swung down at a speed I

hadn't thought possible for something that large. Swift grabbed me and dragged us both to the left as I dropped the shield, narrowly dodging the strike as the massive hand crashed into the floor. There's no way it would have held against an attack that strong.

Yui lunged for it, teeth sinking into the bone. All hell broke loose.

FORTY-THREE

The skeleton reared back, trying to fling Yui off its arm, but she held on, her feet scrambling for purchase. Lopez was trying to sneak up behind the warlock to attack him directly, but whatever magic was emanating from him was keeping her from reaching him.

I charged in, headed for Costa himself. Sliding under Yui's feet, I thrust my blade up at an angle. It struck whatever dark force was creating the skeleton and slid off to the side, sparking as it went. Swift was right behind me, but her mace bounced off with a loud clank, the momentum of the rebound making her stumble.

Costa's dark eyes turned to me, and the skeleton moved with him. Ignoring Yui's attacks, it swung the hand she was attached to straight at me. Instead of dodging, I slid to the side and met the strike with one of my own. The blade of my katana cut through the black flames and into the wrist bone but the skeleton didn't seem to feel pain.

Yui flew over my head as the skeleton finally managed to fling her off. She rolled as she hit the floor. I didn't have time to worry about her before the thing came for me again. I parried the next strike, barely, then Swift was there. She hit the back of its hand and drove it into the floor.

Another explosion rattled what was left of the mansion, and a wave of heat rolled over us. The skeleton faltered for a moment as orange flames battled against black. Fire continued to pour from Danner's hands as he walked slowly forward. The skeleton lifted its hand and swung it down, but Danner batted the attack away with a burst of flames shaped like a giant fist.

"Blackwell," Swift said.

"Yeah?" I debated rushing the warlock again. Maybe we just had to wear it down.

"I'm going full berserker," she said, adjusting her grip on her mace.

"Are you sure that's a good idea?" I asked, stepping away.

It was not a good idea, but we were fighting something that was half warlock, half god, and it was bigger than a damn house. Bad ideas were all we had.

"Just don't get in my way."

Lifting her mace in the air, she slammed it against the ground, shattering the floor under her feet. The air around her was whipped into a frenzy. Debris swirled around her like a mini tornado.

The giant skeleton turned its burning red eyes to her. Swift roared as her magic exploded outward in a massive wave. I was already running toward the warlock himself, but it still managed to knock me flat. Her eyes always glowed when using berserker magic, but they were on fire now. Her skin looked like it was cracking under the pressure as bright pink lines erupted all over her face and arms.

As she lifted her mace, it grew even bigger. Spikes burst out of the sides and pink flames churned around it. "I'm going to crush your bone puppet and give the scraps to my dog!" she shouted, her voice booming around us.

She didn't even have a dog. Not that I was going to interrupt to remind her of that.

"It is you who will be crushed and fed to the hounds of hell!" Costa swung at her. Swift didn't just jump out of the way, she launched herself straight at the skeleton. Magic blazed around her like a comet as she collided with its chest, knocking it back.

It roared in anger and smacked its hand against its own chest in an attempt to crush her. She knocked the hand away and kicked upward, lifted her mace overhead, then brought it down on the skeleton's face, knocking its jaw askew.

Show-off.

"Get Costa while she deals with that thing!" I shouted at the rest of the group as I pushed back up to my feet. Danner nodded, and we both charged in. Yui leaped over me and attacked the skeleton, hopefully buying us time along with Swift.

The warlock shouted something in a language I didn't recognize, and flames fell from the skeleton like raindrops. I slid to a halt as the new magic crackled in the air.

Curling up from the floor all around us like twisted plants were strange, dog-like creatures. The one closest to me lifted its head. It had no eyes, no face, just a mouth that was held open in a silent snarl. Where fur should be was slick muscle, not covered by skin or anything else.

"What the hell are these things?" I shouted.

"Does it matter? Just kill the fuckers!" Danner shouted back as he charged at one, fire racing ahead of him like a tidal wave. It engulfed one of the nasty critters, but it didn't fall. It ran at him, flames trailing behind it. *Shit*.

Lopez lunged at the one closest to her and ripped away a chunk of its throat. It kept fighting, undeterred by the injury.

Another leaped at me. I caught it just below the head

and my katana cut through it like butter. The two pieces of its body hit the floor, black goo spilling at my feet.

"Destroy their heads!" I shouted as I charged at the next. It became a blur of blood and teeth as I cut through as many as I could, but for every one I killed, it seemed like two more sprung up. This was even worse than dealing with the hydra.

Swift slammed into the ground behind me so hard the floor cracked underneath her, leaving a small crater. She jumped back to her feet, but blood was streaming down her face and her entire body was trembling. Berserkers would fight until their body gave out. Sometimes it was their heart, bursting in their chest, other times it was the magic that consumed them. She couldn't keep this up forever.

I kicked one of the zombie hounds and stabbed my blade through the top of its skull. We were fighting a losing battle. It was only a matter of time before we were overwhelmed.

My feet were suddenly swept out from under me as the skeleton's hand closed around me. I managed to cast a weak shield to keep it from crushing me, but the magical flames seared the skin on my back.

Yui lunged at the hand and bit down on the wrist, getting her long teeth uncomfortably close to my shoulder. It grabbed her with its other hand, and she snarled in pain. I pushed against the hand closing around me with all my strength, trying to move my katana into a better position.

There was a sickening crack and Yui wheezed, blood dribbling from her lips. Her eyes met mine for a moment before she was jerked away. The skeleton slammed her into the ground as hard as it could and she stopped fighting back. It did it again and again, her white body flipping like a rag doll.

Screaming in rage, I tried to force the hand encircling me open again. I couldn't let her die for me, even if I did want her to stop eating my Oreos.

It was time for another bad idea. Mayhem magic surged inside of me. Dropping the shield, I pushed the magic out instead. It wrapped around the bony hand and ate away at it. Costa and the skeleton screamed in pain. I guess it could feel *that*.

Its grip on Yui loosened and she fell to the ground, limp. It dropped me, as well. I yanked the mayhem magic back, wary of Costa absorbing it again, but it was a struggle since I'd released it without using my katana as a focus. I was angry, and the magic wanted to destroy everything.

"Look out!"

I reacted before the voice registered, whipping around and cutting through a zombie hound that was leaping straight for me. Breathing heavily, my eyes were dragged upward, toward that familiar voice.

Hiroji stood where the roof used to be. Ice extended from the broken remnants of the wall like a bridge ahead of his steps. His white katana gleamed against the night sky as he lifted it and charged in, bright light streaming behind him like the tail of a comet.

There was no time to wonder what the hell he was doing here. I lifted my arms and let the mayhem magic flow around me while Hiroji was distracting Costa. It destroyed the hounds, burning them into ash.

Hiroji's attack landed on the skeleton's face with a blast of bright magic. Swift hit it in the shoulder with a shout, and the bone cracked under the force of her blow. She continued her onslaught, seemingly determined to remove the arm with blunt force.

Hiroji found me in the chaos and jumped to the ground, finishing off two more of the hounds that had popped up.

"What are you doing here?" I shouted as I ran to Yui's side. She was perfectly still where she lay on the ground. Her white fur was streaked with blood.

"I could feel this thing from a mile away," he said, gesturing at Costa. He dispatched another hound, then turned back to me. These things were *relentless*. "Is she dead?"

"I don't know," I said, touching her hesitantly. She wasn't breathing, which wasn't a good sign. "Did you come to play hero or something?"

"That's your job. I just came to make sure this thing doesn't destroy my house, too." He lifted his hand, and an icy blast rushed past me, freezing a hound in its tracks. "I think the words you're looking for are *thank you.*"

I rolled my eyes. "I'll thank you if you can help me get to the warlock."

There was nothing I could do for Yui right now. If she wasn't dead, she needed a healer. Costa had to be stopped as soon as possible.

Hiroji twirled his katana and thrust backward, catching another hound in the head. "Is that a request for help?"

"Don't push it," I growled. Standing back up, I snapped my katana sharply, slinging off the excess blood coating the blade, then charged Costa. I knew Hiroji would follow. Whether we were speaking or not, he didn't back down from a challenge. And this was one hell of a challenge.

Lopez ran in as well, launching herself at Costa's back as I slashed at the energy churning around him. Mayhem magic slid down my katana, coating the black blade in darkness. If Costa wanted chaos, I could give him that.

Hiroji's bright attack followed mine. We fell into step, moving as one person in a way Swift and I were just starting to be able to do.

The skeletal apparition shuddered above us, and one bony arm crashed to the floor. "One down, one to go!" Swift cackled above us.

If she could beat the skeleton to death, we had a chance. I attacked faster and harder, pouring everything I had into the assault. Fire blazed behind us as Danner kept the zombie hoard at bay.

"I've been waiting for you to fight like you mean it," Costa said, his sunken eyes turning to me. The amulet on his chest began to glow, pulsing every time my mayhem magic collided with his shield.

"Then fight me, you piece of shit!" I shouted, letting the magic wrap around my body. Flipping around my grip on the katana, I punched the shield that had been holding us back. It cracked. I punched it again and again, the mayhem urging me on.

"Logan, stop!" Hiroji shouted, but his voice sounded far away. And who was he to tell me to stop? I had to kill Costa. I wouldn't let the bad guy get away again. I *couldn't.*

Without warning, the shield parted, and I fell into the space with Costa. The amulet flared to life, and all the magic surging around me was sucked into it like a black hole. I hit my knees, but I wasn't going to let him take it without a fight this time. If I couldn't walk, I could crawl to him.

Hiroji was shouting something behind me. His magic

flared, bright and powerful. I could feel it, but it couldn't reach us in here.

Costa looked down at me with a sneer. "Just like you, the rest of the world will kneel once my final sacrifice is complete."

"Like hell they will," I said hoarsely. My muscles trembled with the effort of keeping me from face-planting on the floor. "You're going to die, and no one will remember your name."

He took a step forward, but one of the red marbles Edgar had spilled rolled under the sole of his foot as he put it down. He slipped, just for a moment, but that was all it took.

Costa's eyes went wide, and the shield around us faltered along with his concentration. Lopez surged through a gap, her jaws clamping around his arm. He screamed in pain as she jerked him backward.

I lunged for him. My hand closed around the amulet. The magic inside it burned my fingers. Gritting my teeth against the pain, I ripped it free.

"NO!" he shouted, his face contorting in fear. A spell rushed from his outstretched palm, but Hiroji flashed past me and struck it aside before it could reach its target.

I wrapped both hands around the amulet and snapped it in half.

Power. Chaos. Pain. It surrounded me and poured into me.

The skeletal creature exploded in a shower of bone and flame. Costa faltered as cracks appeared all over his body. Black flames poured from his eyes and he screamed in pain. Swift appeared out of nowhere, falling toward the ground in a blaze of pink. Her mace slammed down on his head, crushing him into a pile of dust.

I caught a glimpse of her expression as she turned to me. She looked afraid.

I tried to reach out, but I was falling. This was a sacrifice meant for a god, but it was being dumped into me. I couldn't contain this kind of power or chaos. It was too much. It was going to rip me apart.

FORTY-FOUR

Swift was shouting something, but her words were lost in the roar of the magic.

A bright light was shining in my eyes. Blinking, I realized it was Yui's body. It pulsed, the light growing brighter and brighter.

The world was spinning, and it was hard to focus on anything. My teeth chattered as my body twitched. It wasn't meant to contain this kind of power.

The moment Costa stepped on the marble kept replaying in my mind even as the power tore through my body. It was such a stupid mistake. An unfortunate twist of fate...for him at least. I didn't know for sure that Fate had intervened, but it felt like he had. It felt like we were being toyed with.

My muscles suddenly seized up as though I'd been electrocuted. Then, the light I'd been seeing abruptly flared out until it was all I could see. Out of it stepped...Yui, still in her kitsune form. Three tails waved behind her.

She rushed toward me, moving so fast she was a blur. She wasn't slowing down. Her paw hit my head and I flew across the room, my leg catching on a piece of debris before I crashed through a wall in a shower of dust and splinters of wood.

Groaning, I blinked up at the rain still falling through the missing roof, confused. That had hurt like hell, but...the magic had stopped. It felt like it was gone.

Yui appeared over me, back in her human form.

"Did you just hit me?"

"There was a bug."

I rubbed my forehead. A knot was already forming. "A *BUG?*"

She shrugged. "I know you don't like bugs."

Swift jogged up behind Yui, still breathing heavily. She was no longer in berserker mode, and she looked like she'd been beaten to hell. Her cheeks were strangely hollow, like she was starving, and her face was pale.

"How did you stop the chaos magic?" she asked, looking back and forth between me and Yui.

"You didn't have to hit me so hard," I complained, sitting up. The room spun around me. "What the hell just happened?"

"I just bound the excess magic collected by the sacrifices deep inside Blackwell's soul to keep it from consuming him and destroying everything in a hundred mile radius," Yui said, yawning and covering her mouth.

"What?" I demanded, looking up in alarm.

"It's fine," she said, waving away my shock. "You won't be able to access it without extensive training, so there's no risk in you blowing yourself up."

"I want it gone. That's black magic. I don't want it sitting in my *soul*," I said angrily.

"Then you shouldn't have broken the amulet like that," Yui snapped, putting her hands on her hips. "I didn't have a lot of options."

I sighed and put my head in my hands. Swift walked over, extending a hand to help me up. I let her pull me to my feet, rubbing my still aching head. "That could have gone better."

"We're all still alive, and Costa is dead. That's all that matters," she said, punching me not so lightly on the shoulder. I stumbled from the force of it, but she grabbed my arm before I could fall over. "Sorry, it'll take me a moment to...adjust."

"That was a warlock?" Hiroji asked, looking at Costa's remains.

"Yes, he's been behind the attacks on New York and Boston," Swift said.

Lopez shifted back, still breathing heavily from the

fight. "I'm going to call Bradley, and a cleanup crew," she said, gesturing at the mess around us.

"The High Chancellor will want to handle the clean up himself," Swift said, her face darkening at the reminder this was her father's house.

Lopez nodded. "Alright." She headed outside, pulling her phone from her pocket.

Swift looked around, then said, "I'll be right back. I need to see if something of mine happens to be here."

We were silent for a moment. I was still reeling from the effects of the amulet.

"This was just like old times," Hiroji said, a rare smile on his face.

Nostalgia hit me like a wrecking ball, but anger followed right after it. "Like old times? Not really. Because now, instead of celebrating together, you're going to scurry back to your father."

The smile left his face, and coldness replaced it. "You'll never be able to just let it go, will you?"

"How could you even ask that?" I clenched my hand into a tight fist. "I can't turn a blind eye to what you do."

"Perhaps you should consider why I do it," Hiroji snapped angrily. "You never think of that. You never *think* at all."

"Tell me then!" I shouted, throwing my hands in the air. "Stop making me guess at everything. Be direct for once, you cryptic asshole!"

"How could you ask me to throw away my family after losing your own? You, of all people, should understand the pain of that. I honor my father."

"There's no value in honoring a man who spills the blood of innocents," Swift said, reappearing at my shoulder. "I should know."

Hiroji laughed humorlessly. "So I should be like you? Live with a price on my head and no hope for a future? Blackwell might have paid off your debts this time, but they'll find another way. You use him as a shield, what do you know of *honor?*"

Swift stiffened beside me. This wasn't exactly how I'd wanted her to find out. I also had no idea how Hiroji knew that, but he had known a lot about her he shouldn't have. Further evidence of the corruption of the Mage's Guild.

"I do what's right. That's honor enough for me," she ground out. "And I will never put Blackwell in harm's way just to protect myself."

Hiroji sneered at her, then turned his sharp gaze back to me. "Let me make this threat once again, but know that this time, I mean it. If you ever step foot on my father's property again, I will take your head."

He turned and walked away, a dark figure disappearing into the destruction that stretched out in front of us like a wasteland.

"Well, that was awkward," Yui said, walking over.

I glared at her. "Shut up."

She narrowed her yellow eyes. "And that's rude."

"Leave him be, Yui. Now's not the time," Swift said as she turned to me and crossed her arms. "Because right now, he needs to explain exactly what the hell he did to pay off my impossibly huge debt."

I took a step back and raised my hands in surrender. "Look, I was just sick of the assassination attempts."

"Really?" she ground out. "And when were you going to tell me what you did?"

"I thought you'd figure it out when they didn't come to arrest you," I said with a shrug. "That was a really shitty plan you had, by the way. Why didn't you just ask for help?"

She dropped her arms. "Ask for *help*? How do you ask someone for that much money? It's insane, and whether you realize it or not, paying it has put a target on your back."

"I, uh, do realize that, actually," I said, scratching my head. "Your father made that clear."

Her face paled, then went red. "What did he do?"

"Just some mild threatening," I said quickly, trying to placate her. "It's no big deal. The Mage's Guild has never been a big fan of me. This doesn't really change anything."

She shoved me, hard. "You're an idiot."

"And you have a martyr complex," I said, shoving her back.

She looked shocked for a moment, then shoved me even harder, sending me flying back. My legs hit the couch and I flipped over, tumbling from the half-burned cushions, to the floor.

"You could just say thank you!" I shouted from the floor, too tired to get back up.

"Thank you," she muttered, her footsteps leading away.

I guess the argument was over. Letting my eyes slip shut, I just stayed on the floor. I was exhausted. Maybe if I just slept for a few minutes...

"What the hell happened here?" Bradley's voice boomed through the house, rattling my brain inside my skull.

I groaned and pushed up to a sitting position. Never a moment's rest on this job.

FORTY-FIVE

A helicopter flew overhead. I looked up, expecting to see the prosaic police, but instead saw the emblem of a local news station emblazoned on the side of it. A reporter was leaning out with a camera, surveying the damage.

"Who the hell alerted the media?" Bradley shouted behind me.

My phone buzzed in my pocket. I pulled it out and saw a text from an unknown number.

```
They won't be able to hide how bad
their shit stinks now ;)
```

I hastily shoved my phone back in my pocket. That had to be Bootstrap. He must have leaked our location. There was no telling what else he gave to the media. I was glad he had, of course, but I didn't want to give Bradley any reason to suspect I was involved.

"I'll try to get rid of them!" I shouted back before hurrying outside. Sometimes running away was the right option.

I crawled over a pile of rubble and headed for the fence that encircled the property. Pulling myself up onto it, I saw that there were over twenty news vans and a crowd gathered outside the estate. A single black limousine was weaving its way through the mob. The small red and black flag fluttering on the hood of the car indicated it was an official Mage's Guild vehicle. We had bigger problems than the media.

Dropping down from the fence, I jogged back to the house. Swift was already hurrying out to meet me.

"We should go." Her mouth was set in a grim line. "Lopez will cover for us."

"For once, I completely agree."

We turned to leave through the back gate, but two black-robed magisters were walking in. More of them were walking through the house, their massive magical signatures pulsing against my brain. The Chancellor's personal guard must be with him, not that he needed a guard. I doubted there was a single mage alive that could defeat him in a one-on-one fight.

Swift tapped my elbow and motioned her head toward the house. I guess we were going to have to face the consequences of breaking in, traumatizing someone under the protection of the Mage's Guild, and destroying the Chancellor's home. I'd really been hoping to put that off for a few days, maybe even avoid it altogether.

The magisters trailed behind us. The back of my neck prickled with the feeling of being watched. I *hated* having an enemy at my back, and that was definitely what this felt like.

Walking back into the now open space at the center of the house, we saw Chief Bradley, flanked by Danner and Lopez, facing off with Lord High Chancellor Swift. Three more magisters stood behind him, their hands clasped in front of them and hoods covering their heads.

"I think your questions can wait until the Mage's Guild can explain why the warlock showed up here at all," Bradley's voice cut through the tense silence.

The Chancellor raised his hands in a placating manner. "There's no need to be so argumentative. We're on the same side here."

"Until the information shared is going *both ways*, I have to assume that the Mage's Guild is opposed to what the IMIB was founded to do; arrest and prosecute anyone using magic to commit crimes." Bradley crossed his thick arms and stared at the Chancellor resolutely.

I was impressed he'd said all that without shouting.

The Chancellor's eyes strayed to Swift as we

approached. He turned his attention back to Bradley and said, "If you'll excuse me, I need to speak with my daughter."

Bradley waved him away and turned back to Lopez, asking her something quietly.

The Chancellor approached us, motioning down the hall, the walls of which were mostly gone. Swift turned and followed silently. I wasn't about to let her go with him alone after all the time he'd spent trying to kill her just to persuade her to fall in line.

She glanced back when she saw I was following and tried to gesture for me to stop. I shook my head firmly and picked up my pace. She mouthed something, and while I couldn't tell what she was trying to say, it was obvious she was trying to talk me out of following. I shook my head again and realized the Chancellor had stopped and was watching our exchange with little amusement.

I walked up beside Swift, who had stopped, and crossed my arms.

She sighed. "Whatever you have to say to me, you can say to him, too."

"Is Costa dead?" the Chancellor asked, ignoring my presence.

"Yes," she said firmly. "He is dead, and the magical item he was using to amass his power has been destroyed as well."

He nodded. "It would have been better to not have this incident take place here, but at least it is done. We will find out who leaked this to the media."

They were always so worried about how things *looked*. I curled my hand into a fist and held back all the snarky comments I wanted to make. I might be brash, but I wasn't stupid. Bootstrap, on the other hand, well...I hoped, for his sake, that whatever he'd done was untraceable.

"Is that all?" Swift asked, keeping her face blank. Despite the calm front she was putting on, I could feel the tension radiating from her.

"For now, though there are some things we still need to resolve. If you need your new *partner* to be present for all our conversations, perhaps we should arrange a dinner," he said.

"Sure, why don't you and your wife come over for tea while we're at it," I said, sarcastically.

Swift gave me a horrified look. "That's not—"

He grinned. "We'll do that."

I ground my teeth together to keep the smile on my face, but I wanted to punch something. "Great."

Just *great*.

FORTY-SIX

About an hour ago, we had finished the initial paperwork and Bradley had ordered us to get out of his way and go sleep. Swift had left quietly for home, but despite my own exhaustion, my mind was restless. Certain questions had been gnawing at me for weeks, and I suspected I knew who had the answers.

Which is why instead of walking up to my apartment, I was standing in front of Master Hiko's door. I knocked once and waited. Soft footsteps sounded from within the house, and the door slid open.

Though I'd been expecting Hiko or Sakura, it was Yui that stood on the threshold. She leaned against the frame acting as comfortable as if she lived there. Not that that meant anything. She did the same thing in my apartment. I couldn't see Sakura letting her get away with leaving crumbs everywhere, though.

Actually, the thought of Sakura stabbing her with a shuriken brightened my day considerably.

"I shouldn't be surprised to see you here," I said, a muscle in my jaw twitching. I wasn't *surprised*, but I was annoyed. She was everywhere. I couldn't discount the fact that she'd almost sacrificed herself to save my life, but I was tired of being in the dark. "You seem to know more about my life than I do."

She rolled her eyes and scoffed at my tone. "Don't take it so personally. I met Sakura and Hiko before you were even born. Of course, back then we weren't exactly on friendly terms. Once I became your guardian, it was only polite to reach out and warn him about the things you were involved in."

"You could have warned *me*," I said, the anger I felt leaking into my voice. "A head's up would have been fantastic, in fact."

Instead of her usual annoying response, she bowed her head slightly. Almost apologetically. "Not without angering Fate."

"Do you work for him?"

Her lip curled up in distaste. "Definitely not. But pissing him off would be stupid. My *giri* won't allow it."

Giri was an old Japanese ideal that didn't translate exactly into English. It was a sense of duty and honor. She felt she had to take every precaution to protect me, even when it conflicted with what she might have wanted. Especially then. Her emotions had to come second to her responsibilities. And pissing off Fate would put me at risk.

"What exactly do you think you're responsible for? Keeping me safe? Or is there some bigger plan at work here?"

"Gods and men are always plotting and grasping for power. That never changes. I don't get involved, and I don't want to. My duty is simply to keep you alive. Don't overthink it," she said, flicking my forehead with her finger.

I rubbed the now sore spot and watched her mistrustfully. "Pardon me for not taking the word of a trickster."

Her lips curled into a smile, but she didn't try to refute her nature. "Go talk to Hiko. I'm not the one that's been lying to you."

She walked outside, her hand brushing my shoulder as though she intended to comfort me. I appreciated the gesture...but should probably make sure I still had my wallet later.

The house was quiet as I walked in and shut the door behind me. My feet traveled the familiar path to Master Hiko's sitting room. It was empty, so I knew I'd find him in the garden. That was where he went when something was bothering him.

The cool night air calmed me a little, but I was

dreading this conversation. All my life Master Hiko had been right. About everything. He didn't make mistakes. He didn't do wrong. The idea that he had been lying to me was like a lead weight dragging at my legs.

I slipped off my sandals by the garden entrance and padded along the path with bare feet. Water rushed noisily along the little creek that fed the koi pond, and a frog croaked from the bushes, but the place was otherwise silent.

Rounding a turn, I saw Master Hiko sitting on a short stone bench facing the night sky. The moon was low and bright tonight.

"Your training paid off," he said, not moving from his spot.

"Did you see the news?" I asked, putting my hands in my pockets as I stopped next to him.

He nodded and took a sip of his tea. "Yui said you and your partner fought well."

"Did she also tell you Hiroji showed up?"

He sighed deeply. "She did not mention it."

I shook my head. At least I wasn't the only one she kept things from. "We both know that's not why I'm here."

"You've come to find out why I've been lying to you," he said, still not looking at me. Setting his cup on the bench next to him he folded his hands in his lap and shook his head. "After so many years, perhaps I should have learned that dishonesty, even when we attempt to justify it as protection, always ends up hurting someone."

"So you're saying you've been lying to me to *protect* me?" I asked, incredulous. "Is this about Fate?"

He waved away the suggestion. "Fate is a problem, but the kitsune is doing what she can to protect you from him."

"She ran away last time he showed up, so I don't know about that." I rubbed my hand across the back of my neck.

He picked up his tea cup again, swirling the dregs around the bottom. I'd never seen him acting this nervous and guilty.

"The night your parents were killed, I could not save them," he said, his eyes going distant. He shook his head. "They were my friends, and we had fought together. We were closer than family."

I curled my hand into a fist and bit my tongue until I tasted blood to keep from interrupting him, but a knot was forming in the pit of my stomach. He could have lied to me about Swift, or about almost anything else...but if he had lied to me about my parent's deaths, I wasn't sure I could forgive him.

"We knew the war was ending, and we knew that

once the treaties were signed, a new leader would be elected." He dropped his head and clasped his hands behind his back. "Your mother was outspoken, and your father was an idealist. They could not be swayed with bribes or promises of power. That is a dangerous thing for a leader. It put a target on their backs."

"Get to the point," I said with gritted teeth.

"I warned them. Sakura warned them. But we didn't know who was behind the threats, and they wouldn't back down. It wasn't until after they were killed that I put the pieces together," he said, shaking his head. "I did everything I could to find allies who would challenge their murderers, but everyone was tired of fighting. They wanted to keep their newfound peace, even at the expense of justice."

"Who was it?" I asked, my voice a little louder than I intended.

He looked up at me, finally. "Swift."

At first my mind went to my partner, but she was younger than I was. It wasn't her. There was only one person it could be. Her father. Everyone knew he controlled the Mage's Guild from behind the scenes.

Anger so strong I could barely breathe rushed through me. My body trembled with barely suppressed magic and violence. That's what the book from Gresham's store had been trying to tell me. It kept flipping to the passage about the Swifts, and I thought that was because I wanted to know who my partner was. But that wasn't it, that wasn't the question I most wanted an answer to. It was trying to show me the truth. "He killed my parents because he couldn't control them?"

Master Hiko nodded. "When I realized there was nothing I could do without simply trying to kill him, I stopped. Your parents wanted you safe, above all else. I had always planned to tell you when you were old enough. Then every year, I found an excuse to put it off. I didn't want to test your control or risk you running off to challenge the Chancellor to a fight you'd surely lose."

I ran my hand roughly through my hair and began pacing. Maybe I would have. Honestly, I was tempted to do that right now. Maybe I could get a lucky shot in and kill him before he squashed me like a bug.

"Hearing your partner was his daughter made it clear how wrong that decision was. You had a right to know much sooner." He stood and turned to face me fully. He dropped to his knees and bowed deeply, pressing his head to the ground. *"Makoto ni moushiwake gozaimasen deshita."*

In English, sorry means sorry. In Japan, it's different. These words combined with his posture was an expression of deep regret generally reserved for your superior. He was humbling himself before me. He was saying he had failed me.

It was like a knife to the chest. But it wasn't enough. I turned and walked away. Angry, hurt, and frustrated.

I barely saw the path in front of me. I didn't bother putting my sandals back on and yanked the back door open, tracking dirt into the house.

Swift couldn't have known about this, but if she had...

No. There was just no way. She was more likely to go after her father than I was if she knew, just like she had with that magical artifact she'd destroyed.

I'd have to tell her about this soon, but I couldn't deal with it right now. All these years of wondering, and now I knew who had killed my parents. Or at least who had ordered it done.

Sakura stood by the front door, barely concealed in the shadows.

"Get out of my way," I ground out, not in the mood for more talking.

"You will listen," Sakura said sharply, stopping me in my tracks.

"To what? More excuses? I have every right to be angry."

"Yes, so be angry for as long as you need. You do not have to forgive us. But when you decide it's time to take your revenge, let us fight with you," she said, her tone lacking its usual steel. "You will need help no matter how powerful you become."

I stared at her for a moment, then nodded. She stepped aside and opened the door for me. I walked out and didn't look back. This place had felt like home, and they had been family, but all of that had just been destroyed.

Never in my life had I felt so alone.

FORTY-SEVEN

"Why are you so cranky?" Swift asked, throwing a roll of paper towels at me.

I caught them and yanked a few off, bending over to clean up the coffee I'd thrown all over the carpet. "I'm not cranky," I muttered.

She rolled her eyes. "Right. You just throw coffee around your office on a daily basis. For fun."

"I don't want to talk about it right now, okay?" I said sharply, as I dabbed at the stain.

Sighing, she joined me on the floor and grabbed a few paper towels, helping clean up my mess. She didn't say anything else, which I appreciated.

After the initial shock had faded from the night before, I realized I had no idea how to tell her I intended to kill her father one day. It was obvious she distrusted her father, but I had no idea if she still cared about him.

Maybe the whole honesty versus lying to protect someone thing was a little more complicated than I'd given Master Hiko credit for.

There was a brisk knock, and Lopez poked her head in. "Bradley wants to see you both."

I threw the soggy paper towels in the trash and nodded. I'd have to get the stain out with a little magic later. It wasn't important right now.

"We're about to get fired, aren't we?" Swift asked as we walked down the hall to his office.

"Eh, fifty-fifty chance we get to keep our jobs," I said with a grin. "We *did* stop the warlock."

She gave me an unimpressed look as she pushed open the door to Bradley's office.

The chief was standing behind his desk, arms crossed, eyes narrowed. "Well, well, my two least favorite detectives."

"Least fav—"

He held up his hand, cutting me off before I could get started. "You blew up the Chancellor's house, managed to attract media attention that has embarrassed the Mage's Guild, and were seen working with a well-known yakuza member on *national television.*"

I cringed. I hadn't realized that had been caught on camera. "To be fair—"

Smacking his hand against the desk, he shut me up again. "No talking! No excuses! And no *explanations!*"

Standing up straight, he cleared his throat and continued. "Costa's case is closed. No more investigating him, or the Mage's Guild, or anyone else. You stay away from his coworkers, and you don't make any comments to the press. Understood? Don't speak, just nod yes."

We both nodded, keeping our mouths shut.

"If you can make it through the next six months without making the Mage's Guild look like a bunch of bumbling, lying, untrustworthy buffoons, then you get to keep your jobs. If you don't, well, we'll all be retiring early," he said, glaring at us intently. "I've stuck my neck out for you two idiots, and you better not make me regret it."

"We won't, sir," Swift said. When I didn't immediately respond, she kicked my ankle.

"Ow," I said, jerking my leg away and glaring at her before turning my attention back to Bradley. "We won't let you down."

"The Mage's Guild is looking intently for whoever leaked information to the media. I assured them it was neither of you." He narrowed his eyes at each of us in turn. "There are many things we would all like to see...improved in the world. One day, we will get to see those things happen. However, it is not going to happen tomorrow, or even next week. Do you understand what I'm saying?"

I didn't like it, but I did get it. Rooting out corruption in the Mage's Guild wasn't going to happen overnight. "Yes, sir. I get what you're saying."

The door suddenly banged open, and there was a high-pitched squeal. I jerked in surprise, but relaxed when I saw pigtails bouncing past my chair.

A little girl who couldn't have been older than four ran and catapulted herself at Chief Bradley. He caught her and swung her up in the air.

"Pappy!" she shrieked and kicked her feet, smiling the whole time.

"Matilda!" A stern woman appeared in the doorway. "I told you not to run off while were at the IMIB. People are working here."

Both the little girl and Bradley completely ignored her. Matilda leaned close to *Pappy's* ear — one day I'd get a chance to mock him for that nickname — and pointed at Swift shyly, whispering a question.

"Why don't you ask Detective Swift yourself?"

Her little face went bright red, but she leaned forward with wide eyes and asked in a shy voice, "Can I see your big hammer?"

Swift grinned. "Of course." Holding her hand to the side she summoned the mace. It glowed brightly, and smoke leaked from her eyes. Matilda cringed away, but when Swift extended the weapon to her, she overcame her hesitation and touched it.

"Whooaaa," she said, enchanted. "It's so big."

"I'm sorry, I hope we didn't interrupt anything important," her mother said, walking up next to me.

"Not at all," I said with a grin. They'd come in at exactly the right time. There's no telling how long we might have been stuck in here otherwise.

"I'm Alyssa, Chief Bradley's daughter, by the way," she said, introducing herself.

I shook her hand. "Detective Blackwell. It's good to meet the source of all the coffee mugs."

She smiled and shook her head. "I thought he threw them all away. I can't believe he actually brings them to the office."

There was a brief flare of magic, and Matilda shrieked again, drawing our attention.

"Here, this one is for you. Just don't hit anything important with it," Swift warned as she handed Matilda a tiny version of her mace.

She took it and waved it around menacingly, baring her teeth and growling fiercely. Bradley had to dodge the first swing before it took off his nose.

"Oh god, she's going to break everything," Alyssa muttered quietly.

I bit the inside of my cheek to keep from laughing out loud.

"Will it last?" Bradley asked, looking as surprised as Matilda.

"Yes, it's small enough that I could make it permanent," Swift said with a smile.

Bradley's face then did something I'd never seen before. It lit up with a huge grin. He patted her on the shoulder. "You two get out of here. I'm going to take my daughter and granddaughter to get ice cream."

"Yes, sir." I nodded at Alyssa, then Swift and I made a quick escape.

We climbed into the elevator and I muttered, "Suck up."

She winked at me. "Somebody needs to keep us on his good side."

FORTY-EIGHT

My apartment was packed. To let off some steam, I'd invited everyone over for dinner. Lopez and Swift were debating the origins of some kind of magical artifact she'd found back before she'd been transferred.

Yui and Danner were sitting in a corner playing a game of Go. I didn't even own that game and had no idea if Yui had summoned it out of thin air or if Danner had brought it. He moved a piece, then glared at her. She moved a piece as well and smirked at him.

He glanced at the board and rubbed his hand along his jaw. "You're cheating."

"Prove it," she said, her smirk growing.

There was a knock at the door and I hopped to my feet, my stomach rumbling in anticipation of food. Takeout was definitely the easiest way to feed five hungry people. It had certainly taken the delivery person long enough to get here.

Checking briefly through the peephole, I saw a young guy in uniform holding three bags of food.

I pulled some cash out of my wallet and opened the door. "Can you bring it in and set it on the coffee table?"

He looked up and met my eyes. Everything stopped. "It's good to have friends over after a close call with death."

Swallowing uncomfortably I looked over my shoulder. My apartment was empty. He had taken me somewhere again. "What do you want, Fate?"

He frowned. "You seem to still misunderstand. This isn't about wanting or needing. It's about destiny."

I ground my teeth together. "Alright, let's say I buy that. Was it the warlock's *destiny* to trip over a marble and die?"

He shrugged. "It was your destiny to defeat him, if you learned how to work with your partner. You did that, and you succeeded."

It was intensely creepy for him to be masquerading as the delivery boy. Especially since he was so young.

"Are you here to give me another task or something?"

"No, just to remind you to focus on what's important. Your petty squabbles with the Mage's Guild will only be a distraction in the coming days," he said as the scene around us changed abruptly.

The air was hot and filled with smoke. We stood on the remnants of a destroyed city. It was unrecognizable, but the smell of death was in the air. "War is coming."

"Am I supposed to prevent this somehow?" I demanded, throwing my hands wide. If this was the future, then I did want to stop it. I just wasn't sure I trusted that this was anything more than illusion and manipulation.

"When you defeated the warlock, you gained something invaluable. Raw power. That *kitsune*," he said, spitting out the word distastefully, "bound the power deep inside you. You must find a way to reach it in order for you to fulfill your destiny and save your world from destruction."

"That power was about to tear me apart. She didn't have much choice if she wanted to keep me alive."

He sneered at that. "She underestimates you."

From anyone else, I would have taken that as a compliment. But I didn't like the way he said it; like I was a tool.

"I doubt that," I said stubbornly. Turning away I began walking through the chaos, but before I made it two steps the scene changed again. But I didn't pay any attention to what was around us.

My eyes were drawn to the figure laying on the

ground in front of me. Her pink hair was longer than it was now and matted with blood the color of her trench coat. The ever-present pink glow of her eyes was gone, they were just dull brown instead.

"What the hell is this?" I demanded, barely resisting the urge to check for a pulse. This wasn't real. Fate was just messing with my head.

"This is what could be if you fail," he said, crouching down next to her body. He smoothed a strand of hair off her forehead, fingers trailing over her pale, white skin. "To be perfectly honest with you, she is not destined to live for very long."

"Is that a threat?" I asked, curling my hands into fists.

"It's a warning," he said, looking up at me. "You will have to learn to let go of what you cannot change. There are more important things to be considered."

I took a deep breath to steady myself. "There is absolutely nothing more important to me than protecting my friends and family."

"How many lives would you sacrifice to save her? A hundred?" He raised one hand, and bodies piled up to my left. "Or a thousand?" He raised his other hand, and a mountain of dead appeared.

"Maybe I can save them all," I shouted at him, fed up with this whole conversation.

"When the choice comes, it will be obvious," Fate said as the whole scene disappeared.

In the blink of an eye, I was standing in my doorway in front of a delivery boy again. My heart was pounding in my chest like I'd just run a mile. There was chatter behind me. I turned abruptly and saw everyone was back in the apartment. The oppressive feeling that always came with Fate had lifted as well.

"Sir," the delivery boy said, clearly repeating himself, "where would you like the food?"

I stepped back, gripping the door tightly to hide how my hands were shaking. "Coffee table."

Yui jumped up from the game and hurried over, digging through the bags to find what she'd ordered. I tipped the delivery boy and he hurried away, clearly freaked out by how weird I'd been acting.

I dragged my hand down my face and leaned against the wall, letting everyone else deal with the food first.

"What's wrong?" Swift asked, nudging my elbow.

I looked at her, surprised at how relieved I was to see her up and walking around. "Nothing, just...tired."

"Alright, we don't have to talk about it right now," she said, calling me out on my lie. "Come eat, you look pale as a ghost."

I followed her, trying to remind myself I didn't believe in destiny or fate. If someone or something was going to try to kill her, I'd find a way to stop it. I had to be able to change it.

FORTY-NINE

The waiter set a tower of trays between us. They were loaded with finger sandwiches, scones, and dainty cakes. Sure, it all looked delicious, but it might all be poisoned.

I still couldn't believe I'd let myself be manipulated into having tea with Swift and her parents. My big mouth had finally gotten me in trouble. Swift was even less thrilled than I was to be there, and I couldn't blame her. I wouldn't want to have tea with people that had recently been trying to kill me, either.

"Are you on course for a promotion soon?" Lady Swift asked as she picked up the teapot and filled Lexi's cup with black tea.

Since her husband held such a high position in the government, she wasn't allowed to hold one as well due to laws against nepotism. They liked to make rules that seemed to prevent corruption, but in fact, did nothing. She still got the title, though. The Mage's Guild fancied themselves paranormal royalty.

Instead of working for the government, Lady Swift was the reason their family was so rich. She ran all their investments and was supposedly the civilian ambassador between mages and other races. In reality, she was more like a prim and proper British yakuza.

My partner added a small amount of milk to her tea, then a single spoonful of sugar, stirring so delicately it barely even created ripples. I had no idea she could be so careful. Normally when she ate it was like someone had set a starving barbarian loose. "Promotions are strictly limited in the IMIB. I transferred in at an already high level, so I won't be eligible for ten years," she said as she gently set her spoon down on her saucer.

Her mother hummed in acknowledgment, but the noise sounded like disapproval. "I see." She turned her piercing eyes to me as she filled my cup on the low table in front of us. "What about you?"

She might have been the one to order my parent's deaths, but it could have been her husband as well. Maybe they'd both even been there. They were powerful mages in their own right, after all. I didn't understand how someone could go from political assassinations to serving finger sandwiches.

I idly wondered if I could move fast enough to kill

one of them before the other annihilated me. Risking a glance at the Chancellor, I remembered being held against the wall in that room, unable to move. I didn't have a chance, at least right now.

I grabbed a finger sandwich off the tower. "I turned down my last promotion. It would have taken me out of the field, and I'm not interested in a desk job."

"I suppose we all have our...talents," she said, raising her eyebrow. Again, in disapproval.

The undercurrents in the conversation were extremely uncomfortable. I shoved the whole sandwich in my mouth and chewed resolutely. Lady Swift's left eye twitched slightly at my inelegant action.

The High Chancellor, who had been silent since greeting us, finally spoke. "The Mage's Guild would like to congratulate you both on your quick and somewhat discrete handling of the recent issue with the warlock. Hopefully, in the future, these sorts of issues can be handled with less...collateral damage, but that does not change our appreciation."

"We'll certainly try to defeat warlocks faster in the future. That will be easier when they haven't had two years to amass power and scheme," I said with a pleasant smile as I added milk and sugar to my tea. I jabbed my spoon into the hot liquid and stirred noisily, letting it clink against the delicate fine china.

Lady Swift's fingers tightened on the handle of her

own cup. Maybe it was a family antique. I hoped it cracked.

"The Mage's Guild is always working to improve communication with the IMIB," the Chancellor acknowledged, but it was clear he couldn't care less about my verbal jab.

Lexi was being too quiet. I didn't like this version of her. She wasn't even glaring at me or telling me to stop antagonizing them.

"I'm sure," I muttered, slouching back in my chair and chugging the slightly too hot tea in one long gulp.

She cleared her throat and finally gave me a *look*. "Detective Blackwell and I have been working together very well. I'm sure in the future that will only improve."

"Ah, yes," the Chancellor said with a grin that made my blood run cold. He pulled out a thick envelope with an official-looking seal. "That reminds me."

I eyed the envelope, immediately suspicious. Anything that made him look that smug couldn't be good.

"As a gesture of gratitude for your assistance to our daughter, and in this case, I wanted to give back a little something. The old estates should remain with their families, not be sold off to anyone that might buy them," the Chancellor said, extending the envelope to me.

I took it hesitantly, his words not quite making sense. "What are you saying?"

"That is the deed to your estate, back in your name as it should be. I appreciate that you were willing to sell it to pay off Alexis' fine, but we wanted to restore it to you. After all, our daughter's mistakes shouldn't be entirely your burden. We share some responsibility for them as her parents," he said, gesturing magnanimously.

Lexi stiffened beside me. Man, these people could make the meanest thing sound so proper. It didn't change the fact that they were assholes. Despite all that, I now had a death grip on the envelope.

I didn't believe this was about relieving some kind of guilt. I didn't think the man was capable of feeling that emotion. Or any normal human emotion, for that matter. To be that power hungry, you had to suppress your human side.

This was probably part of some convoluted scheme, but selling the estate had been painful. It had been my home. It was the place my parents died. If he was going to just give it back, I wasn't going to turn my nose up at it.

"So gracious of you," I said as neutrally as possible.

"We have an appointment with Chief Bradley, so we really need to be going. Is that all?" Lexi asked, her voice strained. The insult had been aimed at her, and it had apparently had the desired effect.

I stood without waiting for their response, and, on

impulse, grabbed a couple of scones just to see Lady Swift twitch.

"Thanks for the house and the tea," I said with a brief nod.

Lady Swift stood and looked at her daughter. "Yes, that is all, for now."

The Chancellor extended his hand for a shake. "Until next time."

I shook it and then nudged Lexi, prompting her to end the staring contest she was having with her mother. The skin on my neck crawled with unease as we hurriedly left. If that had been a battle of words, we'd lost. Badly.

Swift walked with her hands clenched into fists at her side and her mouth pressed into a thin line. We both remained silent until we got outside and into the car.

She sat in the passenger seat, almost speaking a few times before shaking her head. Fed up with it, I said, "Just spit it out."

"You sold your family estate to pay my fine?" she asked finally, glaring at me, which I felt was completely undeserved.

I shrugged. "It was just sitting there not doing anyone any good. So, yeah, I sold it. The Mage's Guild pushes people around all the time. There was no way I was going to pass up an opportunity to screw up one of their plans. And I was really getting sick of the assassination attempts."

She punched my arm, but it was a weak blow. "Don't do that again."

"Don't get fined again!" I retorted, rubbing the spot she'd hit even though it wasn't sore. I didn't want her thinking she needed to try again.

She huffed at my response and looked away. "Thanks, Logan."

"You're welcome," I responded quietly, starting the car.

As we drove away from the Mage's Guild headquarters, my mind kept straying to the envelope in my jacket pocket. Now that I had it back, I realized just how glad I was to not have lost it. Part of me hated the place. It was where my parents were killed. Still...it had been a long time since I'd visited the place.

I should at least check it over to see if the Chancellor had bugged it or sabotaged it in some way. There had to be a reason he gave it back other than just to insult Swift. I'd like to figure that out sooner rather than later.

FIFTY

The ancient wards that protected the estate were still intact, but I doubted they'd ever been this weak before. Magic, like physical items, required upkeep. This place had been neglected for a very long time.

The gate swung open, and I drove into what looked more like ancient ruins than my family estate. The driveway used to be lined with a neat hedge. Cone shaped trees had stood behind it, evenly spaced every few meters.

Now, however, the hedges had grown over the drive-way. The stone was broken in places where roots had tunneled their way through. A tree had fallen, and the rotting wood lay in my path. I stopped the car and climbed out.

The walk to the manor gave me more time to reminisce than I wanted. It was windy today, too, just enough to make it seem chilly outside. The sky was gray overhead, and thunder rumbled in the distance. Leave it to England to rain the first day I'd set foot in the country in years.

The grounds looked more like a forest than a lawn. The pond was scummy, and the exotic fish that used to live in it were probably long dead.

Thunder rumbled again, this time accompanied by a flash of lightning that lit up the old manor. It had been a masterpiece of engineering and magic when it was first built, but now it looked more like the world's biggest haunted house.

Picking up my pace, I made it to the front steps just as it started to rain. I hurried inside without pausing to take in the moment. The wards welcomed me with a warm rush, and the door opened with a loud creak. I left it standing open behind me. Wind blew past me, ruffling the sheets draped over the few pieces of furniture still left in the entryway.

It had been over fifty years since I'd stepped foot in this place. It was musty but cleaner than I expected. The wards must have kept out bugs and rodents even if they couldn't stop dust from collecting.

My memories of the place had faded over time. It didn't feel like home, it felt like a museum. I walked farther inside, leaving behind the patter of rain against the windows. The family portraits still hung on the walls. They had been painted by whoever was the best at the time, which had resulted in a mish-mash of styles. My father had proudly commissioned some abstract artist for his portrait and received a weird, colorful thing that captured his personality well, if nothing else.

I paused next to the first wide hallway I came across. It led to the west wing of the house, which held the banquet hall my parents had been killed in while making their last stand. I'd never repaired the damage, and it still sat in ruin. I doubted I ever would repair it, especially now that my finances were a little tighter than I was used to. With three other wings, it wasn't like I needed the space, anyhow.

Aimless, I paced through the hallways, peeking into long-empty rooms. There was little furniture left. I had sold off a lot of it when I was younger, leaving only my parents' rooms and offices untouched. It had seemed pointless to let it rot in the house unused.

I jogged upstairs and headed toward my father's office. Halfway there, I froze.

I could have sworn I'd heard...

There it was again. A scuffling noise. It wasn't a rat or a wild animal. It was a person.

No one should have been able to get in here. Although, the Chancellor could have left someone behind while he briefly owned the estate.

Putting one hand on my katana, I crept forward, keeping low. They weren't moving like they'd heard me coming, and they seemed to be humming to themselves. It could be a distraction for another assassin — it had been a while after all — or a trap, maybe even a decoy. No matter the risk, I had no choice but to confront them.

I prepared a spell with my left hand, then leaped into the room, ready to draw my katana.

"WHAT THE FU—" a gangly kid stumbled backward over a pile of dirty clothes. He hit the ground with an unmanly shriek and rolled over, scrambling away. "Dude, it's me! Don't stab me!"

"I have no idea who you are," I said, advancing on him with every intent to punch his lights out.

"Bootstrap!" he shouted frantically, hugging the wall. "I'm Bootstrap!"

I paused. He was about the right age, and his voice *was* annoying. "Prove it."

"You're Logan Blackwell, and this is your house that you sold to pay off Swift's fines, but her dad gave it back to you because of some weird, Machiavellian scheme that will never make sense, and I've been working for you for ages, but after I leaked all that stuff to the press, the Mage's Guild got real close to finding me, so I had to run, you know? And this place has been deserted–"

"Shut up," I said, pinching the bridge of my nose

between my thumb and forefinger. Sighing deeply, I looked at my newest squatter. "Speak slowly and succinctly."

"You're even grumpier in person," he muttered, pulling himself to his feet. "I'm hiding out here, and I..." he paused, apparently collecting his thoughts. "I'll give you a twenty-five percent discount if you let me stay."

I glared at him.

"I'll be quiet as a mouse! You won't even know I'm here! And it'll be even easier to consult me since I'll be right down the hall. Or farther away if you want, like, a whole wing to yourself. If you're even going to move back in." He caught my expression and abruptly clamped his mouth shut.

"You can stay, but," I took a step forward and jabbed my finger in his face. "You find shit for me for free."

"Free?" he squeaked.

"Free. And you clean up after yourself. *And* you'll fix and maintain the wards. I know you know how to." If I was going to be burdened with yet another squatter, this one was going to earn his keep.

He opened his mouth to argue, and I narrowed my eyes at him. "Damn, fine. I guess I have other customers," he said with an aggrieved sigh.

"How did they find you, anyhow?" I asked, crossing my arms.

"Well, they didn't, yet. Just got uncomfortably close. It was better to relocate."

"Great," I muttered as I looked around the room. He'd been here for a few days at least, based on the amount of clutter.

He began running around picking up clothes and trash, holding it all in his arms with nowhere to put it. This kid might have been a genius hacker, but he was apparently dumb.

"How old are you again?" I asked, suspicious.

"I'm nineteen!" he insisted. "I know I look young, but I swear I'm an adult."

I rubbed my hand across my eyes and took a deep breath before continuing. "Fine, you're an adult. Do you know if Chancellor Swift did anything to this place before he gave it back to me? Bugged it somehow?"

"Nah, I did a super in-depth sweep when I first got here. No point in staying here if it was just going to get me caught," Bootstrap said with a grin.

At least that was settled. "First good news I've gotten all week," I muttered. "I need to check on a few things. Find a trashcan and clean this crap up."

He nodded and hurried to comply.

Leaving Bootstrap to tidy up, I wandered back out into the hall and looked around. I hadn't ever considered moving back in here after leaving. But, if Yui was determined to keep living with me, it would be nice to have more room. There was a section of the house that was technically the servant's quarters — which sounded so pretentious in this day and age — that I could move into without having to face living in rooms with too many bad memories attached.

It had a kitchen, bathrooms, and everything else you needed to be self-sufficient. There would be room for all of us. Maybe I'd even invite Swift to move in, since she was probably flat broke if she was living off her IMIB salary.

I snorted. I was going to have to rename the place from Blackwell Manor to Squatter's Manor.

Walking slowly, I continued on to my original destination. My father's office. The door handle warmed under my hand as it unlocked and let me inside.

It had been preserved perfectly, unlike the rest of the house. The wards were strongest here since he'd always wanted the place protected. The papers he'd been working on still sat in the middle of his desk. A book with a letter tucked into the pages as a bookmark lay on the old leather armchair he favored.

I walked farther inside and sat down behind his desk. The chair creaked loudly but supported my weight. A silver glint caught my eye, and I pushed aside a pile of papers covering a lump. It was my father's family ring.

My breath caught in my throat. I assumed it had been lost when they were...torn apart. But it had been here all along. Tentatively, I picked it up, turning it over in my hand. There were no jewels set in it like most family rings. It was simple, just a silver band with the crest engraved on the top, which had been pressed into an oval.

I slipped the ring on the third finger on my right hand. It fit perfectly, and wearing it felt like I was reclaiming something I'd given up.

Clenching my fist, I strengthened my resolve. I might not have control over as much as I had thought, but I wasn't going to just roll over and accept whatever Fate said. Maybe I could change my destiny and Swift's. Maybe I could make a difference.

Thank you for reading!

Reviews are very important, and sometimes hard for an independently published author to get. A big publisher has a massive advertising budget and can send out hundreds of review copies.

Leaving an honest review helps me tremendously. It shows other readers why they should give me a try. It also helps motivate me to write the next book even faster!

If you've enjoyed reading this book, I would appreciate, very much, if you took the time to leave a review. Whether you write one sentence, or three paragraphs, it's equally helpful.

Thank you :)

P.S. Join the Facebook group and chat all about the Chaos Mages. I really enjoy the conversations and sometimes it sparks new ideas/ ways to put Blackwell in peril.

P.S.S. Check out my recommendations at the back of the book for more awesome stories.

https://www.facebook.com/groups/thechaosmages

CAST

Logan Blackwell – Logan Blackwell is a long-time agent at the International Magical Investigations Bureau. He is a Mayhem Mage, cursed with a rare and chaotic magic. Blackwell likes to do things his way, and is particular about his cars, suits, and food.

Lexi Swift – An eccentric Berserker Mage, and new IMIB agent. She transferred from the Magical Artifacts division and is now Logan Blackwell's partner. She wears a blood red trench coat, knee high leather boots, and has short pink hair. As a Berserker Mage, she is a formidable fighter, and a little bit crazy.

Chief Bradley – Chief of the Homicide and Robberies Division of the IMIB. A stocky and wide man known for his loud rants and keen intellect. It is suspected the tank is named after him.

Sgt. Lopez – Sergeant with the IMIB, Homicide and Robberies Division. A short woman with dark-brown hair and eyes the same color, and a round face that makes her look approachable. However, she is a determined and intelligent officer that doesn't let anyone push her around.

Viktor – Coroner at the IMIB and a necromancer. He can raise anything from the dead as long as the head is still intact. The Russian man has an imposing presence, a chiseled jaw, and is suspected to have wrestled a bear...and won.

Sgt. Danner – Sergeant with the IMIB, Homicide and Robberies Division. Looks unkempt, and lives by the motto: If it ain't my problem, it ain't my problem.

Master Hiko – An old Japanese mage and master of *battoujutsu*. He took Blackwell in after his parent's death and trained him, teaching him control, and giving him the katana that holds back the mayhem magic. He has a long braided beard which he often tucks into his belt.

Sakura – An old Japanese woman, and ninja. She also

helped raised Blackwell after his parent's death, though she refused to train him citing that he was "too full of chaos to ever learn the way of the ninja". She is scary accurate with shuriken, and often appears and disappears with no warning.

Billy – An employee at Rune Rental in Moira. Billy is in his early twenties, a little bit timid, but loyal to Blackwell. He is always trying to get Blackwell a better car after he inevitably destroys his current ride.

Professor Gresham – Owner of Gresham Rare Books. He has unruly white hair, bushy eyebrows, and thick glasses. Professor Gresham has known Lexi Swift since she was a child and is very fond of her.

Hiroji – A member of the yakuza under his father, and former best friend and childhood companion to Blackwell. Hiroji has dark black hair, a piercing gaze, and a good poker face. He carries a katana, however unlike Blackwell's, it is not used to focus his magic.

Alberto Bianchi – A vampire, and son of Martina Bianchi. Claims to not be part of the mob, but is revealed in Stolen Trinkets to be very deeply involved. Appears to be in his early thirties, despite being about eighty years old. A goatee hides a weak chin and ages him a little.

Sgt. Patrice Jackson – An old mage who guards the records room, commonly known as "The Cave". She is sweet as Southern apple pie if treated right, and vicious as a water moccasin if pissed off. She is rumored to keep the remains of a stupid individual that attempted to force their way into the records room in a jar in her drawer.

Peterson – A clumsy detective that is incapable of watching where he's going or keeping his coffee in a cup. Also an unhelpful coward that no one likes.

Juan Carlos – On the surface, he's an importer. In reality, he's a smuggler. The IMIB hasn't been able to get any solid evidence on him, but his reputation is well-known. He smuggled Costa in and out of Mexico, and is now on the run.

Lady Swift – Lexi Swift's mother. She runs the Swift family investments and is the civilian ambassador between mages and other races. Behind the scenes, she was more like a prim and proper British Yakuza.

Lord High Chancellor Swift – Lexi Swift's father. He is

a powerful mage who holds the second most influential place in the Mage's Guild. Ruthless, power hungry, and not to be trifled with.

Mrs. Schmidt – Samuel Costa's former coworker. She now works in Moira.

Sarah – Victim of the unicorn attack on New York City, and Billy's new girlfriend.

Bootstrap – Runehacker, computer hacker, and informant for Blackwell. He is snarky, charges too much, and has a problem with authority.

Matilda – Chief Bradley's granddaughter.

Alyssa – Chief Bradley's daughter.

Sgt. Zhang – IMIB agent that works in Moira alongside Blackwell and Swift.

Fate – A God, allegedly.

GLOSSARY OF PLACES & FOREIGN WORDS

Magical Revolution – Much like the Industrial Revolution, this merging of supernatural magic and human technology changed the world and spurred both races to new and exciting innovations.

Moira – A multi level city accessible only to supernaturals. The lower levels house the Rune Rail system, and the upper levels are filled with shopping, apartments, and supernatural governing bodies. No one knows how Moira was built, or where it is, other than the mages that created it.

Rune Rail – A train system that travels through a interdimensional portals, taking supernaturals in and out of the city of Moira.

The Edge – Moira is not surrounded by a wall, instead, when you reach the borders of the strange city it simply...ends. The Edge is the place where it dissipates into a strange, murky darkness. A force field prevents anyone from falling off.

Kichijoji – A neighborhood in northern Tokyo, Japan.

Prosaic – The term used to describe human, or non-magical, people in the series.

Runehacker – A mage with the ability to alter, disrupt, or destroy a magical rune. This ability is rumored to be a myth.

Arigatou gouzaimasu – *Thank you* in Japanese. This is the first form of thank you when speaking to someone in a higher social class than you in Japan.

Arigatou Gozaimashita (ありがとうございました) – *Thank you* in Japanese, specifically for something that has happened in the past.

Battoujutsu – The art of drawing the sword. The training is for combat effectiveness through distancing, timing, and targeting. It is not practiced as a sport.

Hadaka no tsukiai – means 'naked communion' or 'naked friendship'. It's a term used to refer to the conversation and experience had while bathing in an onsen naked with friends or coworkers.

Izakaya – A type of Japanese bar with inexpensive food and drinks. It is often frequented by *salarymen* after a long day at work.

Kara-age – Japanese fried chicken. A popular dish at izakayas.

Kanpai – The Japanese word for "Cheers!" in a drinking toast.

Makoto ni Moushiwake Gozaimasen Deshita – A very formal and archaic way of apologizing that would be most commonly used by a samurai.

Onna-bugeisha – Female, Japanese warrior that fought alongside samurai.

Salarymen – A term that refers to Japanese businessmen that work for corporations. They often work extremely long hours, followed by drinking with colleagues and clients.

Tzompantli – A skull rack, generally made of wood, intended for the public display of skulls in Mesoamerican civilizations.

Follow Me

Thank you so much for buying my book. I really hope you have enjoyed reading the story as much as I did writing it. Being an author is not an easy task, so your support means a lot to me. I do my best to make sure books come out error free. However, if you found any errors, please feel free to reach out to me so I can correct them!

If you loved this book, the best way to find out about new releases and updates is to join my Facebook group, The Chaos Mages. Retailers do a very poor job about notifying readers of new book releases. Joining the group can be an alternative to newsletters if you feel your inbox is getting a little crowded. Both options, and Goodreads, are linked below :)

Facebook Group:
https://www.facebook.com/groups/thechaosmages
Newsletter:
https://alexsteele.net/#Follow-Me
Goodreads:
http://goodreads.com/alex_steele

ABOUT THE AUTHOR

Alex Steele is the brainchild of husband and wife team Alex and Stephanie. The persona you see online from Alex Steele is all Alex, but you can find his wife on social media as Stephanie Foxe.

Alex got his itch for writing after Stephanie began to write and publish her series. Previously, he'd never read books (I know crazy, right?). He immersed himself in countless hours of research to better help his wife succeed. It was during that time that he began reading dozens of books and thought, "Hey! Maybe I can do this writing thing too." It turns out writing is hard (who knew?).

What he did learn is that he could outline stories reasonably well and that Stephanie enjoyed writing his ideas. So, Alex Steele was born: Alex comes up with the overall concept, and Stephanie writes it. Alex then reviews it and makes edits. We pass that work on to an editor, then finally to ART (Advanced Reader Team).

We hope you enjoy reading the stories as much as we enjoyed writing them.

Misfit Pack is the first book in a new series by
Stephanie Foxe. Who, if you don't know, is Alex's wife.
She is also basically the one that writes The Chaos
Mages, it's just Alex's idea and she works super closely
with him on it.–

**A redhead with a drawl, a lawyer with pink hair, and
a homeless seventeen year old have no business
forming a pack.**

In a world where magic is commonplace, and your
neighbor is just as likely to be an elf as a troll, three
humans are unwillingly changed into werewolves.

Unprepared and unwanted.

The pack may have chosen Amber as their Alpha, but
that's not a title she is supposed to have. In order to be
legally recognized as an Alpha she must pass the Trials,
and it won't be easy. If she fails, her pack will be

disbanded and forced into a halfway house for bitten werewolves, aka The System.

But the pack needs a sponsor in order to even enter the Trials.

With everything to lose, the brand new pack must learn to work together before it's too late.

The Witch's Bite Series is a complete series by Stephanie that follows Olivia Carter –

We all have our secrets. Mine involves a felony record, illegal potions, and magi–well...the last one could get me killed.

I've been living in a small town working for the vampires for the last six months. All I want is to save up enough to open an apothecary, so I don't have to heal the neckers anymore.

Of course, nothing in my life can be *that* simple.

Two detectives show up at my door asking questions about a dead girl and trying to pin the murder on my employer. Next thing I know, I'm dodging fireballs in parking lots.

The police and the witches want me to roll over on the vampires. The only problem is, I'm almost certain they didn't kill the girl. Although, my best friend and favorite vampire has been missing and won't answer my calls.

Time is running out for me to save my paycheck... and do the right thing or whatever.

www.AlexSteele.net
www.StephanieFoxe.com